LUCY SKYE

THE ADVENTURE OF MAISIE VOYAGER

Jessica Kingsley *Publishers*
London and Philadelphia

4|13

First published in 2012
by Jessica Kingsley Publishers
116 Pentonville Road
London N1 9JB, UK
and
400 Market Street, Suite 400
Philadelphia, PA 19106, USA

www.jkp.com

Library of Congress Cataloging in Publication Data
Skye, Lucy.
    The adventure of Maisie Voyager / Lucy Skye.
        p. cm.
    Summary: Maisie Voyager used to explore the world with her parents but is
living a "normal" life with Aunt Hetty when strangers appear, cryptic messages
are left, and Aunt Hetty is kidnapped, leaving Maisie to try to rescue her
aunt and her parents, as well.
    ISBN 978-1-84905-287-0 (alk. paper)
    [1. Adventure and adventurers--Fiction. 2. Kidnapping--Fiction. 3. Aunts--
Fiction. 4. Buried treasure--Fiction.] I. Title.
    PZ7.S628767Adv 2012
    [Fic]--dc23
                                    2011036866

British Library Cataloguing in Publication Data
A CIP catalogue record for this book is available from the British Library

ISBN 978 1 84905 287 0
eISBN 978 0 85700 604 2

Printed and bound in Great Britain

For Kit
and for Mum, Dad and Edward
You always believed

1

CHAPTER

It all began with Aunt Hetty. She's a scientist, and works in a laboratory. She works for a company that tries to find cures for illnesses and diseases. I'm not allowed to know any details. It's all very top secret. Sometimes she leaves papers lying around and I sneak a look at them, but they're so full of long words that I never understand any of it. I once offered to be a volunteer if they needed any new medicines tested. I thought it would be amazing to see if there would be any side effects, like going blue or having my hands grow to twice their size. It happened in a film I saw! But Aunt Hetty said that they didn't need any volunteers at the moment and she wasn't planning on making anyone turn a different colour just yet. I didn't really mind. I'm not all that keen on medicine; not keen on taking medicine, that is. I don't want to be a scientist when I'm older, not a medical one at least, although I wouldn't mind working with animals. But there are lots and lots of things I want to be more and after what happened recently, I think I'd make a very good detective or a secret service spy. Undercover Agent Maisie Voyager.

I am Maisie Voyager, and I am twelve next Tuesday. I live with my Aunt Hetty in a tall town house, one of the four-storey ones with sixteen windows (not counting the one in the attic roof). My room is right at the top on the attic floor, and from there I can keep an eye on everything that goes on nearby as I look out at the front and back. Aunt Hetty's bedroom and study are in the basement, and then everything else is in between. We have a bathroom each, although I share mine with spiders sometimes, and there's a pigeon that perches on the windowsill when it's open. (I think he wants to make friends with my old rubber duck.) So it's not completely my own, but I'm the one that keeps it tidy. The kitchen is big and old. Aunt Hetty likes old-fashioned things, so there's a wood burner as well as a huge kitchen Aga as well as an electric cooker. She says she likes a challenge. I think it's easier to cook on a fire than it is in an oven but I can only do that when she's there, 'just in case'.

Aunt Hetty makes sure she sees me every morning and evening even though she works such long hours. She makes me breakfast, and I cook her dinner, apart from on Fridays when we go out to eat. I like cooking, especially experimenting with different food, and Aunt Hetty's very good at eating everything I make her. She wasn't very keen on the beetroot omelette I did, but then neither was I. I just thought the beetroot would turn it an interesting pink colour. I get all of my recipes (apart from the ones I make up in my head) from a huge old scrapbook that lives in the kitchen. Aunt Hetty's stuck in all of these recipes that people have sent her from all over the world. It means that on one page you can have instructions for Moroccan goat stew and on the next it's a recipe for Jamaican octopus sandwich. If you're not concentrating properly when you're cooking, you can mix up the recipes. I've learned the hard way. I love the scrapbook though. Reading it reminds me of everywhere I've been and everywhere I've still to go.

I was cooking the evening when Aunt Hetty's visitor came. Onions were spitting a tune at me in the cast iron frying pan, and I was chopping up tomatoes when the sound of the doorbell rang throughout the house. It's an old-fashioned bell pull with sixteen knots in the rope (the same number as there are windows) and the deep clanging of the brass bell reaches every corner of the house, which is handy for when I'm in the far reaches of the attic and Aunt Hetty's in her basement. When I heard the noise I got up from the table and went over to the window, which was open to allow the smell of cooking onions to escape. Leaning out, I looked down to the front doorstep, and stood there was a tall man, dressed in a long dark overcoat. He was too far in the shadows to be properly lit up but when Aunt Hetty opened the front door, the beam from the porch light spilled onto him, and I saw that his coat was actually a cloak made from thick, dark purple material. My face began to hurt. Purple tastes like the bitter grounds of over-roasted coffee. I can't wear anything purple and I hate seeing it. Aunt Hetty knows never to buy me anything in that colour. Most of the time, if I see it, I can try to distract myself by thinking about something else, but if it comes along unexpectedly my brain and jaw freeze and seize. I took a breath and concentrated on the rest of the man, trying to breathe the sour taste away. The cloak was a proper old-fashioned one, like rich people used to wear to the opera, and he carried a parcel under his arm, wrapped up in brown paper. To be honest, it looked ridiculous. Not only was he dressed up like a pantomime villain, the summer evening was so warm I felt like sweating just looking at the thick layers he was wearing. Thinking about pantomimes and silly comedies, I began to feel a bit better. The hood of the cloak obscured his face, so I didn't know whether I knew him or not, but Aunt Hetty obviously did, because she took his free hand and held the door open for him to enter. Before she shut the front door, she looked up and saw my face sticking out of the second-floor window. She frowned, and motioned with her hand for me to go back inside, then slammed the door shut. I ducked my head back into the kitchen, and then ran to the door, quickly opening it to listen to what was going on downstairs. All I could hear was footsteps descending the wooden basement steps; Aunt

Hetty must have been taking him to her private study. The house was suddenly quiet, as the shutting of the study door kept any further sounds from reaching my ears. The only noise left was the fizzing of frying onions.

I took the pan off the hob, heaving its weight with both hands. Most of Aunt Hetty's kitchen equipment seems to be about one hundred years old and made of heavy cast iron. I like heavy objects. Flickery feathers, lace, sheets of paper fall out of my fingers. I'm not clumsy; I just can't always feel them. They're there with my eyes but not in my touch. So pans and books and big woolly blankets are great as I know where I am with them. I took the pan away from the heat and the noise of frying subsided. Silence. Not even the sound of voices. It was very strange. Aunt Hetty didn't often have unexpected visitors. Sometimes friends would pop round but she nearly always brought them up to the kitchen to chat. Occasionally she would hold work meetings at home, but she usually told me in advance, so that I knew what was happening, and then you could hear the raised voices and arguments all over the house (often well into the night). Those late-night discussions were always quiet mumbly chat and then loud guffawing laughter, the sounds of which would waft up to my attic room as I lay looking out of the skylight above my bed. Although they were serious, and about important medicines and research (or so I picked up from the snippets I heard; my hearing is super good sometimes) there was always a happy atmosphere. An atmosphere where your head isn't always worrying about what might happen next.

Not like now. Now, the quiet was worse than any noise would have been. Quiet can be a bit like a light feathery weight; I just don't know where I am with it.

I suddenly couldn't stand it any longer, and hefted the pan back onto the stove. Once all of the ingredients were in the pan, I left it bubbling, making sure that it wasn't too hot so the tomato sauce didn't jump up and splatter the walls. Aunt Hetty didn't like red-spotted wallpaper, and I wasn't too keen on cleaning. One weekend I spent two hours and fourteen minutes getting food stains off the ceiling when kidney beans exploded, and that was enough to make me extra careful. I went back over to the window, and hopped up onto the window seat, my back resting hard against the wall. A draught blew in, catching my hair and sending it flying around my face. As I shook my head to clear my view, I caught sight of something I hadn't noticed before. Maybe it hadn't been there earlier but, because I wasn't expecting it, it automatically seemed to fit in with the other strange events of the evening.

All of the houses in our street are large (some with more than sixteen windows, and some with fewer) and have their own driveway and garage, so you hardly ever see cars parked in the road. If there's a party you might, but even then, some of the houses are so big that there's room on the drive for ten or even twenty cars. Aunt Hetty's small scooter was in our driveway by the rhododendron bush parked when she'd come back from work, but down at the end of the gravel drive, parked across the entrance and blocking the way in and out of the house, was a large, expensive-looking car. Expensive-looking in the old, big, black leather and shiny silver way. The paintwork gleamed even in the twilight. It was so unusual (one that would turn heads whenever it went) that I felt it must have something to do with Aunt Hetty's visitor. I peered at the windows, but could only see blackness; there didn't seem to be anyone in the car. As I was watching, the door to the driver's side opened, and a tall man climbed out. The car hid most of his body, but I could see his shoulders and his face as it looked right up at me. He had a big beard that covered a lot of his face, and long dark hair and, as I stared at him, his glasses winked back. I hate glasses. They stop me seeing people's faces properly and if I can't see their face, I don't know if people are staring at me or looking at something else or frowning or smiling or anything. Slowly, the man raised his right arm and pointed his hand. Light glinted off a large, sparkly ring. He kept on pointing, and I began to feel uncomfortable, backing away from the window to avoid the empty glasses, eyes and finger. My tummy was really tight, and the purple tastes had already given me a head hurt. Suddenly, I realised I was leaning back too far, lost my balance, and tumbled in a heap onto the floor. By the time I'd picked myself up and looked out of the window again, he was gone. It was only because I felt so knotty inside that I knew the encounter had really happened. I screwed my face up into frustrated and heard the door close. The cloaked man was leaving. He scuffled gravel down the driveway, opened the door to the car and got in without once looking back. I was right! The car did belong to him, but I still hadn't had a chance to see his face. The driver put the headlights on, catching a cat in the gleam, startling it out of its mouse-tracking. It scampered away as the engine started with a roar, and suddenly the car was off, racing down the road, the distant view of its taillights growing fainter and fainter until I could no longer see them.

'Maisie! Get back inside!' Aunt Hetty's voice crashed in my head, startling me off the window seat for the second time. As I inspected my knees for dust and bruises she came over and pulled the window closed, although I noticed her taking a quick glance out before she pulled down the blind, shutting out the evening, or perhaps shutting out the events that had just occurred.

'Who were they, Aunt Hetty?' I asked as she bent down to pull me to my feet. She brushed me down before answering, frowning. I thought the frown must be about my appearance. My hair must have been even wilder looking than usual, having been blown around by the breeze, my T-shirt was grubby at the cuffs with the day's dirt, and my knees showed the wear and tear of close collision with the floor. I can get tidy in the mornings, but I lose track as the day goes on. She shook her head and tutted.

'Look at the state of you, Maisie! What are you like?'

'Aunt Hetty! What about my question?' I said, getting annoyed.

'It was just business…work. That was all. You know I can't talk about it.' She turned away and went to the stove.

'But they didn't look like the people you usually work with. They're normal looking, and the man in the car certainly wasn't. And what about the other one? He was dressed up like...like...The Phantom of the Opera... only without a mask and...'

Aunt Hetty interrupted me. 'What man in the car?' she turned round sharply.

'Oh, the driver. He had a beard, a big one, horrible glasses, and...' I frowned, remembering the flash of light as he pointed at me, 'and a big ring on his right hand.'

Aunt Hetty stared at me, and then looked away. I saw her eyes go empty and I knew her thoughts weren't here.

'Aunt Hetty,' I began again.

She came to. 'Maisie, enough. It was business.' Her voice was firm, but I noticed that her hands were shaking slightly. Something was definitely wrong, but I also knew that when Aunt Hetty said 'enough' it meant 'enough', so I decided to leave things for the time being. I would have time to mull them over on my own. People don't always do what I expect, but if I know them, I know when they're being different. Aunt Hetty wasn't being normal Aunt Hetty. I didn't like it.

Later that evening I sat in my room. The night was too warm for a fire really, but I'd started a small one in the grate; more for company than anything else. It made the room smoky, but I like building sticks into pyramid castles, and it reminded me of campfires when I was small. Aunt Hetty had gone to bed early claiming a headache. I wondered if my head hurt had moved to her, so I didn't ask her any questions, just gave her the obligatory kiss on the cheek before making my own way to my room. Kisses taste like pepper. If I expect them, they're quite nice but if I don't they're too hot. I want to sneeze or rub my face free. Goodnight kisses are generally alright.

CHAPTER 2

That evening was the first sign that anything was wrong in Aunt Hetty's life but, by the time the next morning came, the strange events of the night before seemed so distant it was hard to believe that they had even occurred. Yesterday was then. Now was now. I hadn't slept well, though, tossing and turning under my pile of blankets until eventually I gave up and read until morning arrived. Then I washed and dressed, checked my mirror-me was looking as it needed to, and went downstairs, unsure as to how Aunt Hetty would be. She was rushing around getting ready for work just like her usual self.

'Morning, Maisie, honey or marmalade?' she asked as I entered the kitchen. Her long dark hair was tied back off her shoulders, a voluminous apron covering her smart white work shirt and grey stripy trousers. I liked her hair tied back. I could see her face properly, and didn't get worried her hair would try and creep onto me if she gave me a hug. I looked over at the toast to check how black it was. I have toast every day but Aunt Hetty, in keeping with the lack of modern appliances in the rest of the house, has no toaster, and instead grills bread on the top of the Aga. The Aga didn't always work properly and Aunt Hetty was absent minded when cooking, so my morning toast inevitably ended up incinerated on at least one side. I had learned to cope with most of it, but the crusts tended to subtly disappear into my pocket when her back was turned to feed the windowsill pigeon. If I left them on my plate, I had to eat them.

'I've left a shopping list on the fridge, and there's some change in my study if you need it.' Aunt Hetty said, taking off her apron and draining her last mouthful of coffee. 'What have you got on today?'

'Change of what?'

'Oh, sorry.' Aunt Hetty shook her head. 'Spare change, coins and money.'

I coughed, dislodging a toast crumb that had stuck in my throat. She asked me again, 'What have you got on today?'

'Um, well the shopping. And I need to go to the library. For my project.'

'Oh yes, your project. How's it coming along?'

'Aunt Hetty, you know I haven't started it yet,' I said, exasperated. 'I can't decide what to do it on.'

'I didn't know, that's why I asked, but maybe if you look at enough books an idea will come to you.' She came to face me and gave me a hug and then picked up her briefcase that sat next to the fridge.

'Lunch!' she exclaimed, looking around.

'By the cooker,' I said, munching toast and holding out an apple from the bowl on the table to keep her sandwiches company. 'Bye and see you tonight. No one's coming over again are they?' I quickly asked her as she was walking out the door. There was silent space and then she called back,

'No. It was just a one-off meeting. I told you.' Her voice tailed off as she neared the front door. 'Nothing to worry about.'

The door slammed a farewell.

I wasn't worried, but I wondered if Aunt Hetty was from her reluctance to talk. I sat back in my chair and pushed my half-eaten toast away. The day stretched out in front of me, and I looked out the window. Blue sky, clouds that looked like popcorn; perfect for exploring. I had made it my mission this summer to discover every corner of the town, walk down each street and through every park. Before I started, I made a long, long list of everywhere I wanted to see. I was at number seventy-four on my list and had fifty-five to go. It was proving to be a longer task than I expected. Maybe today would get me closer to my target. I had told Aunt Hetty the truth. I would go to the library later, and then do the shopping, but first I had more wandering to do.

On my way out of the house, I looked closely at the space where the car had been parked last night in the hope of finding a clue that would reveal more of the mystery of the visitors. But there was nothing. No scraps of paper or unusual objects, just dirt, leaves and the lonely feather from an unlucky magpie. Straightening up I shaded my eyes, squinted at the sun, turned left and began to walk.

CHAPTER

At this point I should probably explain who Aunt Hetty is, and why I live with her. Although this story is extraordinary, there are many more that I could tell about my life before I came to live in this town. Words are made up of twenty-six letters and letters go in lots of orders. In my head they all tell a very clear story, but out loud other people get confused. Aunt Hetty says people like to know the 'big picture' but I get distracted by tiny, tiny details that are fascinating to me, but uninteresting to anyone else. Hearing about my narrow escape from a hornets' nest when there were over 250 hornets chasing me into an apple orchard with forty-eight trees, or the time I got stuck up to my neck in a wallowing hole for two hours and twenty-two minutes and I had to sing *Nellie the Elephant* 158 times to myself to keep myself calm before I was rescued, is apparently not what people really want when they say 'So, tell me about your childhood.'

No one really tells the 'me' story more concisely than my dad. Never a man to beat around the bush (is what my mum says), although I say he's literally beaten lots of bushes in his time. He says it how it is. And how it was.

So, imagine. You are sitting with me and with my parents. We are roasting or toasting our tired feet around a campfire in the desert. The night is black, but the moon is nearly full and the stars are so many even I can't count and it feels as if the sky goes on forever and ever. In the distance you can hear the call of a wild dog, howling to his pack, and a shiver runs right through you. But then you turn to face the fire again, and look at the glow of warmth on all our faces. And turning to my dad you say, 'How did we end up here?' And he would say...

'When I was young, just bigger than you but not as big as Maisie, I got lost in the woods. They were only near my home and I'd been in them many times before, but this time, this time, the dusk fell earlier than I expected. And the trees grew taller. And the shadows husked darker. And the woods I knew went away and I was somewhere I had never been before. I ran from tree to tree, trying to find some familiarity in the branches and the trunks. But the trees felt wrong, the brambles snared my feet, and I flew into the earth where I lay, shaking, scared. I was only five minutes from home, but I could have been a million miles away. I gradually eased my breathing. I shook myself down and told myself that I was never going to get anywhere if I didn't get myself out of there. I had to treat myself like a soldier. Into mission mode I went, and although I went around in circles for a bit, after a while I managed to orientate myself and find the path. And find my way out of there.

'That evening, I knew that I had discovered something amazing. We never know where anywhere is really like until we have experienced it completely. And so I decided that I wanted to know more about the world and the places that people rarely went. I needed to know everything I could about the planet that I lived on. I was going to become an explorer!

'I met Margaret when I was halfway up a mountain somewhere in the Himalayas twenty years later. Neither of us knew exactly where we were; we both just knew that we were headed upwards and wanted to reach the top. Margaret was twenty-five and I was, well, let's just say I was a little older and greyer. We finished our climb to the summit, and by the time we reached it, six days and three ice falls later, we realised that we had each found a kindred spirit. Or, as Maisie calls it, "a person who knows you most". From that point on, we travelled everywhere together. I was making my living as an explorer for various groups, and Margaret had been working as an anthropologist at the Natural History Museum. Oh, an anthropologist? That's someone who studies how people live. So by joining up together, I could discover more about the land and environment, and she could discover more about the people. We made, and do make, a good team.

'This isn't too dull is it? Good, well, continuing on, for several years we went all over the world, to swamps, ice floes, mountaintops and ocean floors. One month we could be picking nutmeg crops in the forests of Borneo while attempting to document the animal population of the Kapuas Mountains, the next we could be swimming amongst the islands of Tonga, identifying local fish and sea life. It wasn't all fluffy animals and sun holidays though. Once, we were nearly kidnapped by guerrillas in Peru, while we were working with the Andean Indians. Maisie thought I meant gorillas when I first told her, and couldn't understand why we weren't disappointed that we hadn't been taken by the animals. It was only later, when I explained that guerrillas were men fighting against the government, that suddenly the idea didn't sound so exciting after all.

'And then Maisie was born. I think it was somewhere in the middle of a jungle, but I forget exactly where. What? Oh, it was in Bolivia. After a few days rest, we simply wrapped Maisie up in a papoose, and continued on with our expeditions, only with a baby on our backs. Maisie, why don't you continue?'

With the darkness still around us, you turn to me, and I take up the tale.

'As I grew up, nothing changed. We began to stay in places a little longer – I think my short legs slowed down the trekking pace, but I kept up with them as best as I could, with two steps to every one of theirs. Sometimes, they could hire a llama or a donkey to carry me along, and they never wanted to leave me behind. But then, just over a year ago, while we were in Madagascar during the February rainy season, my mum caught a fever. Dad and Palo, one of the expedition assistants and nurse, treated her as best as they could, but eventually the medicine man from a neighbouring village had to be kayaked over to help. He stayed with her for fifty-two hours, never leaving her tent. I could hear chants and humming while I watched from my perch with a lemur in the overhanging tree. Occasionally Palo would open the tent flap, taking in or out strange small bundles wrapped in leaves or cloth. I didn't eat the whole time the man was there and one morning very early, the lack of sleep and food made me forget to stay awake and I fainted, falling out of the branches. My dad picked me up and took me into the tent where I lay next to Mum. He sat in front of us both and told me. She was well. She would recover. But he had been thinking...'

Suddenly, you blink. And we are not around a campfire. There are no dogs, no clear night sky. I am just a small person in a small room in the attic of a town house with sixteen windows (and another in the attic).

I flew here on a plane that had rows of seats in three and five and three. It was very, very big. And they stayed in Madagascar, but only briefly until they moved on somewhere else. They had chosen their life, but didn't feel it was 'fair' to choose mine. They wanted to give me a chance to experience 'normal' life. And only then, when I had spent some years away from them, going to school and living in a stable household, could I make the decision to return. They send me letters and postcards when they can, but post is not very reliable in uninhabited areas of the world. Mum said that they would come and visit, depending on the schedule and where they would get sent to next. But it seems unlikely so I don't plan for it; Mum and Dad are not comfortable surrounded by sofas, newspapers and clothes boutiques. They are much more at home with a water hole, leaf bucket and small fire made from animal dung.

I didn't want to leave, but I couldn't argue, not with Mum so weak, and my dad with his determination face, eyes like river pebbles and mouth just a sad line… I was so, so scared though. Scared in my tummy twisting so I couldn't fit any food or drink in. Scared so that my hands were little paws; I couldn't see my fingers. Scared of everything being different but everything being the same. I liked moving to new places with the same people. I didn't want to move to new people and stay in the same place. It was all topsy-turvy.

So I am here. Doing normal things like going to school, and trying to understand why I need to make friends with people rather than insects and animals. Currently my best friends are the bathroom spiders, so I haven't done very well on that front. It's not as easy as you'd think, and I haven't taken to living in one place. It's the first time I've tried to live a normal life, and it's taking some getting used to. Animals don't talk, so you don't have to translate them, that's why I find them easier. People don't mean what they say. Palo and the other assistants on the trips were straightforward. They talked science and facts. They talked to me without me needing to concentrate on what they meant. I get so tired here, trying to understand faces as well as what's in their heads.

Aunt Hetty is Dad's sister. That's why she wanted to take me in. I'd only ever seen a grainy photograph of her before I came to stay, showing a sixteen-year-old plummeting through the air leaping off a diving board. I didn't believe it was the same person, as I didn't know she would be older now. I expected the same person as the photo, not the middle-aged, longhaired, slightly hippy-looking aunt that met me at the airport. She recognised me though, so we managed to find each other. There were times afterwards when I think she wished she hadn't. I've taken a while to adjust to life here, but we've learned that there will always be ups and downs. If I am going to live amongst people, cars and tower blocks, I'd rather be living with someone like Aunt Hetty than anyone else.

Anger is like being in the middle of nowhere with nothing underneath or above or around. You reach out and up and down and nothing. Then you feel spinny and dizzy and loopy and lost, lost, lost. When I first arrived here, I was so angry. I was angry at being left, angry that I had to live with someone I didn't know, angry that my parents were continuing on their adventures without me. I used to attack the sofa and hit and hit and hit the cushions. It made me feel safe. I could squidge the soft fabric and feel the lines of stitching on my skin. It made me know where I was. I still do it sometimes, but now I'm not as angry. I've come to understand why they made their decisions. Aunt Hetty explained to me that there was pressure on them to further their explorations into more dangerous territories, and they didn't want to risk my safety in perilous situations. As much as I want to be out there with them, I know that their work is incredibly important, and that they have to go where they're told. I worry for them; sometimes I get scared that they'll disappear and we'll never know where they've gone, but I believe that, one day, I will go and join them again. I get periodic crackly telephone calls, where we manage to shout a few sentences at each other before the line gets cut off. So I hoard the few bits of communication that find their way over here. There are twenty-four letters and two postcards that Mum and Dad have sent me, and a wad of brown parcel paper that had carried a pound of dates from Tunisia (dates taste like sunshine smiles), all in an old biscuit box under my bed. The comforting smell of custard creams and shortbread helps to reassure me when I read, and re-read, their words to me.

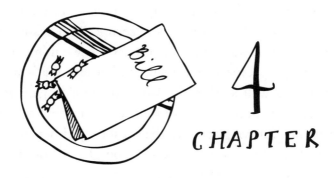

CHAPTER 4

Aunt Hetty behaved in her normal, tired, slightly scatty yet caringly nosy way that evening, and the four evenings following. I was unable to forget the events of Tuesday night, but they had begun to fade to more of a distant memory. We went out as usual on Friday night; the only change being Aunt Hetty's decision to opt for a restaurant on the other side of town, rather than the one we usually went to, only ten minutes away. Aunt Hetty professed a desire to try some prawn linguine rather than onion bhajis and samosas. She told me about it that morning, so I had the day to get used to and think about the idea. I like doing different things. I just like knowing it's going to be different beforehand. She gave me a menu to look at so I could see what food there would be. I'd done so much exploring that day that by seven o'clock I was starving and ready to eat anything that was put in front of me. Aunt Hetty did what I usually did when she was locking the front door, checking not only twice but three times that all of the locks were secure. That made me wonder if she was worrying the house wouldn't lock and strange people would come in, because that's what I think. As well as that she went to the side gate and inspected the bolt, and as we walked down the drive she gave quick furtive glances to the shrubbery either side of the path, as if she expected to see a burglar hiding there, waiting to break into the house the moment we'd left. It was only when I started thinking hard about it that I realised these were probably her exact thoughts.

Once we had left the drive and begun to walk down the road, Aunt Hetty began striding confidently forward like her usual self. She would occasionally glance back over her shoulder, or peer inquisitively down side roads as she passed. I didn't know what she was looking for, but whatever it was never materialised and we kept moving forwards. Aunt Hetty talked to me to keep my mind from getting lost in my head. I spend lots of time on my own as it's what I like best, but it means I sometimes find it hard to come back and start talking to people again. This makes me stressed, so Aunt Hetty knows now to talk to me when we're going out, so I can concentrate on listening to that. She was telling me about the latest medical trial they were performing.

'... And when I went to check on her two hours later, she'd fallen fast asleep into the testing food bowls, and there was mashed potato everywhere! The side of her face was all green from the food dye we'd used too. Apparently she was kept awake last night by foxes at the bottom of her garden, but it means that we've now got to start the tests all over again.' Aunt Hetty chattered away as we crossed the street.

'Green potato?' I asked, only half listening, and then something caught my eye. On the other side of the street a car had pulled up to the kerb and stopped. The windows were dark, and the paint was gleaming – in a way that reminded me of something. I looked harder. The shape, the colour, it was the same! I knew I had only seen it briefly in the evening dusk before, but I was suddenly certain that this was the same car that had been outside our house on Tuesday night. The driver's window slowly began to move down as I watched but stopped halfway, so that only the eyes and top of a head could be seen. It turned and familiar glasses stared over at me. He abruptly raised his hand, the ring flashing again as he pointed out of the window in my direction, and then suddenly, as quickly as it had opened, the window moved up, obscuring his face, and the car pulled out into the traffic. Two horns hooted as the car cut in front of others. Aunt Hetty was seemingly oblivious, continuing to talk about mashed potato, until I grabbed her arm.

'Aunt Hetty, the car!' I exclaimed, pointing back down the road. She stopped, and followed my arm. Too late. The car had merged into the others and was indistinguishable in the midst of traffic. Aunt Hetty frowned, unsure of exactly what I was getting at.

'Any particular car, Maisie? Or all of them?'

'No. It's gone now. But I'm sure that I just saw the car that was outside the house the other evening. When you had your,' I paused, unsure exactly how to put it, 'meeting.'

Aunt Hetty stopped walking and turned me to face her. Again, I noticed that her hands were trembling. 'You, young Maisie, have an overactive imagination. Even if it was the same car, what does it matter? It's not as if they're following us around, is it?'

It was my turn to stare at her, and some things clicked into place in my head. I hadn't considered that anyone might be following us, as I knew no reason for someone to do so. But Aunt Hetty had obviously thought about it, which was why she was constantly looking around her as she walked along, and maybe why she had been so worried about making sure that the front door to the house was locked. If someone was following us, they would know when we were out, and could get into the house without anyone seeing. Thoughts whizzed around in my mind making me very confused. I knew I needed to think it all through properly, but I couldn't do it with Aunt Hetty here. I would have to wait until later when I was alone. I knew I needed to make an excuse.

'Okay,' I said to her, 'Sorry, I've just been reading too much at the library, spy books and stuff. I think it's all got a bit mixed up in my head.'

Aunt Hetty looked at me with wide eyes, unused to my suddenly agreeing with her, but she was obviously so relieved that I wasn't going to argue that she didn't say anything more. And with good timing, for as we began walking again, Aunt Hetty pointed down the end of the street, to the restaurant sitting back from the road where we were going to eat dinner.

Because the weather was so good we sat outside, which was much more interesting for me because not only did I have the other diners to surreptitiously inspect while they were slurping on their soup, I could also watch the passers-by. Like Aunt Hetty said, I do have an imagination (although I don't think it's overactive) and one of my favourite things is to watch people and try to imagine their lives. They become people from books I read; I like seeing words become bodies and faces. I think it's because I'm so unused to seeing so many people of such different appearance all at once. When I was with my parents, we used to go for weeks in the jungle with hardly seeing anyone, and now I'm inundated with images and ideas as soon as I step outside the front door. Books and words let me understand things at the speed my head wants. I make people's lives up rather than asking them lots of interfering questions, and that means I don't have to talk to them. It's much more fun to envisage someone sitting at the next table as an escaped con-man, on the run from prison after being locked up for selling pretend masterpieces that he painted himself. And who was now making a living as a painter and decorator until he could access the money he had hidden away and fly off to the Cayman Islands to begin a whole new life. While in reality he was probably a health insurance salesman, out for the night after spending his day off decorating the kitchen in a new, stylish colour for his wife. It was much more exciting to know them inside my head than in reality – sometimes I wondered if they would agree. I had to be careful not to look at people for too long though because I didn't want to seem rude. I am not always very good at judging how long you should look, as monkeys never cared if I stared at them for hours and I presumed people wouldn't either. People don't like it if you stare at them for more than two or three seconds! So I had perfected my powers of observation by training myself to see as much as possible in a single glance – it was partly why I'd been able to remember so much about the man in the car, and why I'd been able to identify him again much later.

But now it was time to choose some food; I would have time enough to think about the man later. A glass of coke and a bottle of wine had already appeared in front of Aunt Hetty and me, and Aunt Hetty's head was bent over the menu, so I focused for a few moments and realised I should choose something to eat. Aunt Hetty spent ages deciding, and I glanced around the restaurant while I was waiting, identifying a potential trapeze artist, undercover nun and French garlic grower. Once Aunt Hetty had given her requests to the waiter, she sat back, glass of wine in hand.

'Go on then, Maisie. Who are we sharing the restaurant with tonight?'

It was customary for me to share my observations (however wild and fantastical), although occasionally Aunt Hetty would actually know the person in real life, and fill me in on their true profession. Tonight, out of our usual setting on another side of town, Aunt Hetty knew no one, so I could let my imagination wander as freely as I liked.

We talked and talked, and by the time we had moved onto dessert Aunt Hetty had lost some of the little crinkly lines around her eyes that showed she was worried, and was beginning to relax. Putting down her spoon, she excused herself and ventured into the restaurant towards the bathroom. I busied myself making designs in the smears of ice-cream that were left on my plate. Strawberry became swirls, chocolate a crisscross, and I was just beginning on the walnut-flavoured wiggles when a voice suddenly came from behind me.

'Your bill,' a man said, putting down a small silver dish over my shoulder on which was a folded slip of paper and four foil-wrapped mints. I picked up one of the sweets and turned around. There was no one there, just two women eating salads and talking loudly about expensive hairstyles at a table a few steps away. The waiter who had served us earlier was pouring wine for a man who was seated by the entrance. I supposed it must have been him who had put the plate down, but he'd have to have moved pretty swiftly to cover the distance from here to the door. Aunt Hetty still wasn't back, so I decided to open the paper. It wasn't a bill. Well, if it was, it was unlike any other I'd ever seen. The paper was plain, with just a few sentences on it. They said:

AN ANORAK HAS ONE; THERE ARE TWO IN A KNOCK,

THE NEXT IS IN TOY BUT NOT IN A TOCK,

THE THIRD IS IN NEWT, A WARNING AND PLAN,

AND ALSO IN UNDERSTAND THIS IF YOU CAN.

THE FOURTH CAN BE CAUGHT IN THE MIDDLE OF CAT

AND IN A FAT RAT WHO'S WEARING A HAT.

THE FIFTH IS IN NUT, AND ONCE FOUND IN NEWS,

THE SIXTH IS IN CHALLENGE AND THE BEGINNING OF CLUES.

THE LAST CAN BE FOUND AT THE END OF THIS NOTE, AND ALSO THE LAST OF THE LETTERS I WROTE.

NOT UP IN THE MOUNTAINS, BUT DOWN BY THE SEA,

IS WHERE YOU WILL FIND THEM - G, M AND P.

I stared, trying to understand. The big black capital letters glared back at me.

'Maisie? MAISIE?' Aunt Hetty's voice broke through my thoughts. I looked up. Aunt Hetty was standing by the table, looking at me questioningly. I handed her the note wordlessly. Aunt Hetty read it and frowned.

'Did you write this?'

'No! Someone brought it over to the table. I thought it was the waiter, but it doesn't make sense. I couldn't see anyone else who could have done it though.'

Aunt Hetty had been listening intently while I explained things to her. Then she read the message again. This time, something obviously happened in her head because she suddenly crumpled the paper in her fist and threw it onto the table. Her jaw was clenched tight, in a way she looked when she'd had a long, hard day at work. I saw her staring round at the other tables, her eyes moving from one to another to another diner.

'Maisie. Listen to me.' She spoke sharply. 'You must forget this note. It's just a silly, silly joke. There's no sense in...' She broke off as the waiter came over with the real bill, presented on a dish like the one earlier, along with some more sweets. There was no wonder I had mistaken the note for the bill. I was silent while she paid, sucking on another mint. When we got up to go, I quickly slipped the screwed-up message into my pocket while Aunt Hetty's back was turned. I wanted to understand what it meant, something I could only do by studying it further. Aunt Hetty showed no sign that she had noticed what I was up to, and left the restaurant without a backward glance. I had to run to catch up with her quick footsteps.

She kept up the rapid pace throughout the walk back home. Down side alleys or along main roads, even walking over the zebra crossing, she was always one step ahead of me, avoiding any talking opportunity that could be created by us walking together. Similarly, as soon as we were through the front door, there was a quick kiss on my cheek, and then only a waft of her jasmine perfume lingered as she whisked herself off to bed. Although I was slightly disgruntled at such a brisk end to the evening, I was also secretly excited by the fact that I would finally have a chance to think over the week's strange happenings and decipher the mystery note.

But tiredness got the better of me, and I must have dozed off, because suddenly I awoke still fully dressed, my head nodding over the crumpled paper that I had attempted to smooth flat. The sky was dark; there was no pink sunset left, and due to my carelessness three playful moths were chasing each other around my lamp, having entered through my open window. Shooing them out and pulling the window firmly down I changed into my pyjamas, and then shuffled out to the bathroom, needing to get rid of the taste of garlic from my mouth before I finally settled down for the night.

Once on the landing I saw that the hall light was on, so I crept down the stairs, leaping over the creaky step to avoid waking Aunt Hetty. My dance down the stairs was pointless, for as I reached the bottom, I realised from the voices I could hear coming from the basement study that Aunt Hetty was still awake. Not only awake but with company. I checked my watch: it was two-thirty in the morning. She sometimes kept odd hours, but not usually as late as this. I stood for a moment, unsure of what to do next, when a loud crash suddenly made up my mind for me. It was more like a huge bang than a smash, but whatever actually caused it, I knew that it came from the room with Aunt Hetty in it.

I pattered softly down the next flight of stairs and came to a halt outside the thick oak study door. Luckily, it wasn't pulled tight shut, which is why the sounds from inside had managed to reach me upstairs. I crept up to the crack in the door. I could see the shapes of two people facing the fire. One was Aunt Hetty, the other...a stranger. Or at least, a stranger that I thought I had seen before, recognising the deep, dark cloak that was thrown over the arm of the chair. A large wooden chest stood between them and, as I watched, I saw the stranger reach deep inside it and bring out an armful of papers. I could not see the stranger's face, as he kept his back towards the door. Aunt Hetty's face was strange, a mixture of fear and anger twisting her features, and her hands were clenched by her sides. The stranger suddenly raised his arm, lifting his hand, beckoning to the chest. She somehow seemed to understand what he wanted, because she slowly reached down into the chest, removed some more papers and took them over to him. While I had been watching, this had all been taking place in silence, but suddenly the stranger spoke.

'You know what will happen if you don't do this.' The voice was hoarse, but not deep, and very quiet. My ears strained to catch the words he spoke. It was Aunt Hetty who made the noise, replying in a cry that bordered on a shout.

'But why them?' There was desperation in her voice, rising in pitch as she reached the end of her question.

Her body was tense, and she stood stiffly through anger, but there was no answer, just a repeat of the pointed finger. Aunt Hetty's shoulders slumped as she resigned herself to the stranger's whim. She unloaded several more bundles from the chest before he was satisfied, a heap of papers stacked by his feet. The stranger returned to the box one last time, looked inside (maybe checking it was empty?) and dropped the lid. It fell with a crash, echoing the sound that had startled me so much earlier. Aunt Hetty turned away and went and sat on top of the closed chest, her head bowed. The stranger stood still. After a moment's silence, Aunt Hetty raised her head.

'Go.' She said, quietly but firmly. 'You've done what you had to, I understand that, but you must go.'

'I will. But you have to understand, I may be taking the papers, but it's not finished. There is still more that has to be done.' He began to turn away towards the door, as if to leave. I suddenly realised I might be caught crouching in the doorway. Unless I acted quickly, my spying would be discovered, and I had no urge to find out what the consequences of that would be. I spun away, darting quickly up the stairs and into the hallway. I heard the whish noise of the study door opening fully and understood that the stranger would soon be at the front door. In my haste to run up the next flight of stairs I forgot to be careful about the squeaky step. Near the top, my left foot sank into the wobbly board and came back with a loud creak. The footsteps below me stopped, pausing at the sound, but I continued to flee, escaping into my bathroom and balling myself under the sink, trying to calm my breathing to a more even pace. It was going in in in in in in. And I had to remind myself to breath out in out in out in. I wrapped my arms around my knees, curling up my toes and tucking my head down into my lap in an attempt to make myself as small as possible. The fixings under the sink were leaky and cold droplets of water decided to drip down my neck, making me jump and shiver in my pyjamas. Finally, I heard the front door close, and the noise of Aunt Hetty fastening the bolts and turning the key. I sat for a few more moments and then unfolded my cramped legs painfully and left the bathroom. The house was in darkness. I heard no sounds, not even the noise of a car pulling away, and I realised that this time the stranger must have arrived (and departed) on foot. It was like the end of a chapter in a book, and so I thought the excitement must finally be over for the evening. I felt so tired now and it was all I could do to climb the last few stairs to my attic room, pull the covers off my bed, and climb underneath them. I worried about Aunt Hetty. Her face, it had no smiles, no eyes that showed happiness. It looked like the ghost masks from carnival time in Brazil. It looked pale and lost. I drifted off into sleep.

CHAPTER 5

Because of my late-night ramblings, Aunt Hetty had already left for work by the time I dragged myself out of bed, bleary-eyed, and shuffled my way into the bathroom, still trying to pull my clothes on as I walked. One foot bare, the other cosily socked, I splashed some water onto my face and hair, flattened it down to what I'd been told was an acceptable style of smartness, and by the time I made it into the kitchen I was fully clothed and alert enough to face the day. And Aunt Hetty. But although the day was still there, Aunt Hetty was not. The only remnants of her earlier presence were a half-drunk mug of coffee and a few lonely bran flakes submerged in some dregs of milk. I took my time over my own breakfast, squeezing an orange into juice (my prolonged efforts creating a centimetre of fluorescent liquid), scrabbling in the freezer for a bagel and then lightly and carefully toasting it before slathering it with honey. Coffee, or rather a latte, as they would have described it in a posh coffee shop, ended my breakfasting perfectly, and I wondered why it was that cooking breakfast for myself was much more indulgent than when Aunt Hetty made it for me. Most people seemed to prefer others to make food for them. While I ate I filled in the crossword at the back of that day's newspaper. I didn't have a clue to most of the answers; my challenge was to simply find words that all fitted together in the shape provided. Today, I filled in the last of the blanks with 'coconut', deciding my way was much more fun and much more satisfying – you were practically guaranteed to finish it all unless you absentmindedly inserted an 'x' or 'q' somewhere where only words of make believe would do. As I finished this, however, I saw that my food preparation had created enough mess to get a grumble from Aunt Hetty unless I cleared it away. The sink filled up with soap bubbles and hot water, and I pulled on an enormous pair of cerise rubber gloves and a lime-green apron (lots of happy colours make my eyes whizz in a good way) and began piling the crockery next to the sink. This was when I saw the torn notepaper clinging milkily to the underside of Aunt Hetty's cereal bowl. Sighing, and hoping that this was not another note that I would have to spend brainpower deciphering, I read it through. Well, it was readable, if a little blurred, and although its instructions were clear and understandable enough, it only caused me to question the peculiarity of last night's cryptic poem, and all of the further strange happenings.

Maisie,

Sorry to have missed you this morning, sleepyhead, but when I looked in on you (and prodded you) your only response was to roll over and carry on snoozing. Have a good day today, and don't let your brain jump to ridiculous imaginary conclusions. The poem last night was a silly joke and not worth fretting over – I'm not! A new project has come up so I will be working late over the next week – up early with the birds, and in with the bats, but if you do cook, save me some and I'll eat when I can. Sorry to leave you like this, but I will still be here even if you don't see me very often. Think of me and the multicoloured potatoes! Will communicate with you through notes, but if you need to call me at work then do so.

Stay safe, and keep busy,

Lots of love,

Aunt Hetty xxx

Initially, I wasn't sure how to respond to the detail that I was practically going to be home alone (even if Aunt Hetty would be here at night as long as things at work were okay), then I realised it was perfect! I could investigate the cryptic note and mysterious stranger and Aunt Hetty wouldn't know, because she wouldn't be around to check up on me! But where should I start? I began considering the various options as I finished washing and tidying away, but as I stacked the bowls into the cupboard my eyes involuntarily moved to the calendar on the wall. It was Saturday 15th July, and in big scrawling letters that I had written two months ago it said 'Ms Davies' class' and there was an arrow through the following days until the next weekend. Dina Davies ran art and craft courses throughout the summer holidays and, intrigued by the idea of trying woodcarving, batik or glass painting, Aunt Hetty had let me sign up for a week's tuition. But to start the classes today? I dithered, but only briefly, for as much as I wanted to become an undercover sleuth, I didn't have any real idea that I could be successful in uncovering the mystery of Aunt Hetty's strange visitors and her subsequent behaviour. I wanted to go and paint the stars, build the stars, uncover the stars and see what I, Maisie Voyager, could do by myself. I checked my watch, nine-thirty. That left half an hour to run across town to the art-studio/waste-ground/ sculpture-park that Dina called her home. The wild and fantastical creatures that would suddenly appear one day, peeking out of the undergrowth around the building, were what initially captivated me. I had discovered her house on one of my many travels around the streets and, despite my desire to find new places, I kept finding myself returning to her world. One day a eucalyptus tree could have all of its leaves painted different colours, and on the next a rainstorm could have blurred the paint, and dribbled it so it merged in rainbow colours on the branches, trunk and grass underneath.

'Nature adapting my art', that was what Dina called it. I just found it entrancing and stood for hours looking at it all. My visits must have been obvious to her for some time before she ventured out of her studio to talk to me. I was chatting to a silver unicorn who had his head just poking through the bay tree (carefully pruned to look like an ostrich) when I saw her approaching. She waved at me, patting the unicorn's metal tail and making it clang, so instead of quickly making my retreat, I stayed, although I decided to postpone my conversation with the sculpture until later. Not many artists are dressed in the stereotypical way of fairytales, but Dina was. With her long flowing dark hair, paint-splattered tie-dyed shirt and red velvet skirt cut into perfect pixie Vs at the bottom, you knew, as soon as you looked at her, that there was no other profession she could have.

'Hi!' she called, still waving, pink and blue Indian bangles twinkling and jingling on her wrist. 'I see you've met Bessie then?' She expertly pulled herself over to meet me in her wheelchair. It was just another extension of her. Like her clothes, it was covered in paint, bells and knotted ribbons around the handles. The spokes on the wheels were woven with (expertly removed) multicoloured thread, becoming wonderful cobwebs. You didn't see Dina and a chair, you just saw Dina.

'Bessie?'

'The unicorn. I named her after Bessie Smith, an old blues singer. I tend to name most of my animals after the music I listen to when I'm creating them.'

And that was that. In I went, and she showed me round the jungly maze of plants and art work. I went again the next day, and this time she showed me her studio, filled with paints, pastels, half-finished wall murals, pieces of driftwood and odd lumps of metal and clay soon to be re-formed under her skilful hands. I liked Dina. I didn't need to try to understand her; I just did. And she didn't mind if I talked, or if I didn't. And I especially liked that she liked bright colours too. That was when she told me about the art courses she ran, and asked me if I wanted to come along. I didn't even need to consider my answer, and I knew Aunt Hetty would be pleased that I had found something to keep me occupied for at least part of the long summer holiday.

I quickly stuffed my satchel with some fruit and a few odd scraps of paper I had done scribbly doodles on over the past few weeks. Sketching and drawing didn't really interest me though; it was the big creations that I wanted to make. Locking the front door three times for safety, I began to jog down the street, my satchel bumping against my bare legs. The day was humid and sunny, so by the time I reached Dina's my forehead was sticky with sweat and my T-shirt felt damp against my back. Hot and cold are funny things. Hot is sometimes a cuddly thing, and at others like a buzzy fly you can't swat. Cold is like breathing in the mountains and your lungs feel as big as a balloon. This hot was a bit fly-like, but when I stopped running it got better.

I wasn't late, as I thought I might be, but five minutes early, so Dina poured me a tall glass of home-made lemonade and we sat on her front steps, waiting for the others to arrive. I had peeked into the studio as she was fetching me my drink, hoping I wouldn't see it set up with several easels surrounding an unappealing still-life of an apple, old shoe and glass bottle like we got at school, but I was in luck. There were simply several tables covered with different paper and card, and all kinds of art materials. In the middle stood a sign, 'Use anything, use everything. Make something that's your own.' Fantastic! I had been worried that although Dina was so way-out and creative, we students would only be taught the rudimentary basics of drawing, things like perspective and shading. But Dina had come up tops; it was everything I wanted it to be – and more! The week would be one long exploration of imagination.

Dina talked to us for a while once the others arrived, explaining that although she could help us use certain tools, or make suggestions and give advice, this week was all about our work. I knew straight away that what I wanted to do more than anything was make a totem pole, like I'd seen when I visited the Native American tribes in Indiana, so I began to sift through Dina's wood and scrap corner, searching for inspiration. I wanted to make a totem pole because then I could create lots of imaginary and mythical creatures to go on it, instead of having to choose just one. Although, ideally, it would have been best to carve and shape a tall tree trunk, Dina said that a week was not enough time, so I settled for papier mâché, moulding animal shapes from wire and coating them in paper, sticky glue, and more paper, around a tall chunk of wood higher than my head. There were two other children in the class with me. Fred was obsessed with witches, gothic moons and bats, and spent his time intently covering a huge canvas with his mystical creations. Jessica, on the other hand, only wanted to paint small, neat flower pictures. Dina persuaded her to try some pottery, and she began to make some weird lopsided pots that she then painted her intricate floral designs on to. We all talked a little bit, but we seemed more contented just getting on with our work on our own. It was a companionable place for me as I didn't feel like I had to chat or pay attention to someone else's words and face. For the first few days I went home sticky with wallpaper paste, and newsprint, everywhere from the soles of my feet to the hair on my head, and bath time became a chore rather than relaxation. Towards the end of the week, however, I progressed to the painting stage and, although this was just as messy, it at least provided a more colourful tinge to the bath water each night.

One week after I'd begun, Dina and I carefully carried my sculpted, painted and varnished totem pole into her garden. She'd told me I could take it home, but I wasn't certain how it would fit in Aunt Hetty's house, or her small back garden with its neat tubs of pansies. It was much more suited to the fairytale surroundings of Dina's jungle. We eventually decided on a spot not too far from the unicorn and next to the eucalyptus tree that was currently sporting dozens of dragonflies made from aluminium bottle tops on its branches. Stepping back, I realised that there was nowhere else this peculiar-looking column of eagle, bat, a creature that was a cross between a bush baby and a racoon, topped with a wolfish foxy grinning face, could ever have looked in place.

'Perfect!' Dina and I said together.

'Come and see it any time, and bring your aunt, I'm sure she'd love to see what you've been up to. It really looks amazing, you know, Maisie.'

My cheeks got hot, like when you're in front of a fire, and my insides felt like a smile. I was very satisfied with my work, and was glad that Dina approved too.

That week was one of the best I'd had since leaving my parents. Working from ten until six every day left me so exhausted I had no time to think about anything else except the project I was working on. I barely saw Aunt Hetty; our communication was based on scribbled notes hastily written on the backs of receipts and food packets. I didn't have time to miss her and, more importantly, I didn't have a moment to think about the peculiar and strange events of the previous week. Their urgency and danger disappeared the further away they became. And that was my mistake, because they hadn't gone away, they simply lurked like a crocodile just under the surface, barely visible until it suddenly lunged for its prey.

CHAPTER  6

That last evening I walked back home, tired and paint-splattered for the final time. I hoped that Aunt Hetty would take some time off tomorrow and come and see my work. She said this morning that she'd try. She said this by actually writing on the back of an old receipt for daffodil bulbs and a hideous yellow garden gnome she'd fallen incomprehensibly in love with. Luckily, she'd forgotten about the gnome soon after buying it cheap at the nursery, so I had relegated it to the far depths of our back garden where it could moulder happily next to the compost bins. Maybe, I considered hopefully, she'd even be home tonight, so I could tell her all about it.

I'd wanted my work to be a secret and hadn't given her the slightest clue to what I'd been slaving over. I didn't have any real idea as to what she'd been doing all week either. I knew the potato masher had disappeared from the kitchen drawer a few days ago, but we hadn't met, hadn't spoken, and hadn't even been out for our regular Friday night meal, which virtually never happened. This all left me feeling slightly strange. There were things that anchored me safe to my life with her, and they were gradually disappearing.

I stopped off on the way back home to buy myself an ice-cream, feeling that I deserved a reward for my hard work that week, and also wanting something to cool me down from the muggy evening air. The choice 32 Flavour Parlour offered was huge (it really did offer thirty-two flavours) and, being indecisive at the best of times, I spent a good while working out which one was going to be the tastiest, as well as would last me the longest. In the end I opted for a chocolate ice-cream, studded throughout with honeycomb, one of my most favourite things to eat in the entire world. Change jingling in my pockets, satchel swinging on my back, I wandered through the rest of the streets on my way home. The paint on my hands gradually transferred itself to the cone, making a multicoloured smudge pattern. I considered keeping it as a piece of art, but hunger prevailed, and I had just eaten the blue-smudged tip when I reached Aunt Hetty's drive. No scooter. She wasn't home. I checked my watch – seven o'clock. It looked like I would be eating alone again tonight. As I scrunched my way up to the house, a man stepped out of the porch. He had been standing in the corner under the shelter, next to the black boot scraper that was only used when Aunt Hetty and I went for one of our hill rambling marathons. He was dressed extremely smartly, in an impeccably cut and very expensive-looking grey suit, starched white shirt, blue striped tie with its knot in the exact centre of the collar, shiny black lace-ups, and hair greased down without a strand out of place. He smiled as I approached, and I smiled back, assuming from the polished leather briefcase under his arm that he was a salesman of some sort, and thinking that he must be friendly.

I reached him, wiped my hand on my shorts to get the stickiness (if not the paint) off, and shook the hand he held out to me. He continued smiling as I said hello. And then I realised. The smile didn't reach his eyes; his mouth was fixed in a cheerful grin, but the eyes were dead fish eyes. Cold and dark. I stopped smiling, but his smile remained and he began to speak, his eyes the only thing that kept me from becoming drawn into his conversation, and drawn to him. The words he spoke, their content, made me realise that crocodile of unease that had been happily submerged for seven days was beginning to resurface. Not aggressively, not rapidly, but it was gradually making its presence known again. And with it came my confusion and fear.

'Well, hallo there!' He said it cheerfully but it sounded like he was talking to a toddler, not to someone my age. 'I was hoping that someone would be home soon. I've come to visit with Henrietta and I was sure she said to come at seven. We're old friends...from school,' he added as an afterthought. It was like every single one of my brain cells suddenly woke up at once and went 'ZING'. My inside head vibrated. No one, not even Aunt Hetty's boss at work, called her Henrietta. Occasionally the name appears on letters from the bank or council, but that's it. To everyone she's simply Hetty and always has been, ever since my dad gave her the nickname when he began to talk. If this man really was an old friend from school, there was no way he would call her by her full name. I frowned at him, so he smiled wider, obviously trying to beguile me into believing his tale of lies.

'She's not here.' I wasn't telling an untruth, but he looked at me suspiciously. I carried on, 'She's very busy with work at the moment, and I've no idea when she'll be back. It could be ages.' I looked at him meaningfully, hoping he'd take the hint and go away. I wasn't in luck.

'Well. I'm sure she said seven; I know she wouldn't want me to leave without seeing her. Not after travelling so far.'

'How far?' This came out a little rudely, I admit, but I didn't trust him. I didn't know what to do, for Aunt Hetty wouldn't let me invite unknown people into the house, yet he proclaimed not to be a stranger. I resigned myself warily to the fact that I would have to stick with courtesy, however much I was suspicious of him.

'Far.' He answered me, giving no indication to exactly how far or even where he had come from. 'And do you know what I'd love?' I waited. 'A fine, strong cup of tea.

Perfect for reviving me from my long journey.' He had left me with no choice; if he wanted a cup of tea, I would have to invite him in.

The man waited while I pulled the keys out of my bag and unlocked the front door. He entered the hallway and paused as I said, pointing to the coat hooks and empty umbrella stand, 'Would you like to leave your briefcase here?'

'No, no.' He said quickly. 'It's best left with me. You know…' his voice trailed off, and he coughed nervously.

I didn't know, but wasn't sure how to reply, so I led him up the stairs to the kitchen. I made sure he followed me closely, although he tried to peer unobtrusively round the corners of the doors to the other rooms. When we reached the kitchen, I pulled out a chair by the table for him to sit on, and went over to the sink.

Rinsing and soaping my hands under the running water I worked out a polite sentence and said, 'You'll have to excuse me a moment. As you probably noticed, I'm all paint covered. I need to clean up before I put the kettle on.'

'Yes, yes.' He said absently, hardly noticing that I'd spoken, his eyes roaming around the room, taking in the china on the dresser, big green Aga and baskets of apples, potatoes and onions in the corner. I kept an eye on him as I filled the kettle from the cold tap and set it on the Aga top.

'We'll have to wait a while for the water to boil,' I apologised. 'It always takes a long time with fresh water. When we're in, we usually keep one heating constantly, to save time.' I realised I was rambling because I was nervous, and shut up abruptly.

'I had planned to meet with Henrietta in her study; it may be more appropriate for me to wait there.' He looked up from the chequered tablecloth he had been closely examining.

'I thought you said you were just visiting, not having a meeting,' I retorted quickly, glaring hard at his hands. I didn't want to glare at those dead fish eyes so his hands seemed next best. 'And she never lets anyone into her study without her being there as well.'

'Quite so, quite so,' he said in the irritating way he had of repeating words over and over. 'I was very wrong to suggest it. You must excuse me.' He ignored my query about the meeting or visit, deliberately so, I believed. There was silence for a moment, and then I turned, opening a cupboard to remove mugs and a teapot. I decided the plain blue mugs would do, rather than the fine china cups we kept for visitors we liked. The teapot matched the mugs, except for having a chip in the spout where I had knocked it against the tap when I was washing up too enthusiastically one day. In went two tea bags. The room was so quiet; I could hear the faint burble of the kettle beginning, at last, to heat up.

The man suddenly spoke, 'So, so…how long have you been with Henrietta.'

I decided that if he could be cagey with his answers, so could I.

'A while. Would you like a biscuit or some cake, there's home-made fruit cake or digestives?'

'Some cake, I think, would be perfect. Henrietta always was a good cook. It will be lovely to try some of her own baking again.'

This was such an outright lie that I nearly dropped the cake tin onto the floor. Aunt Hetty may be able to cook a little, but bake? Her baking always turns out like plasticine or concrete because she can never concentrate on the recipe for long enough to follow it correctly. Baking was possibly my favourite thing I discovered when I moved in with her. It's like making magic – you put this and that and that and this into a big bowl and (if you get it right) when it comes out of the oven it smells and tastes like tickles. It's all sweet and lovely. If there were any cakes made in this house it was by me. Aunt Hetty had told me that her mother, my grandmother, was as hopeless a cake baker as she was and they'd always had biscuits or shop-bought pink and yellow angel cake when she was a child.

'Well, how long is a while?' He asked as I carefully cut a slice of cake, making sure he didn't get a bit with too much brown sugar or glacé cherries in – the best bits. I put it on a plate and placed it in front of him.

'A while,' I said again. Well, if he could repeat things then so could I. Suddenly, the kettle let out a piercing whistle, drowning anything further that he said. Usually, I'd rush over to the Aga, desperate to stop the piercing noise; however, today it stopped any more talking. The constant 'peep' was still irritating, but at least it stayed on the same note. When Aunt Hetty and I had gone shopping for a new kettle three months before, she was determined to get a traditional whistling one and was tempted by a shiny red model that played 'Polly Put the Kettle On' when it boiled. Luckily, I managed to persuade her that if she truly wanted authenticity in her kitchen, she should settle for the plain black one. So we still ended up with a kettle that 'peeped', but at least it didn't play songs. Songs can get stuck in your head and I don't like that.

I saw the stranger screw his face up in irritation at the noise and decided that I couldn't torture him or myself any longer. I heaved it off the hob and poured water into the teapot.

A few words drifted over as the noise of boiling water died away, '...painting pictures?' I gathered he must have been referring to my splattered state, but as much as he had already irritated me, I took even further objection to his condescending tone.

'No. I haven't. I've been making art.' I told him, deliberately plonking his mug of tea down hard in front of him. It didn't spill, but he jerked back at once, afraid that some of the liquid would splash onto his pristine shirt. He took a bite of cake, carefully licking his lips and freeing his fingers of crumbs. I stood watching him. I knew I was looking longer than was polite and it was beginning to make him uncomfortable. But I didn't care.

After a sip of tea and a gentle clearing of his throat, he spoke again. 'Hmm, delicious. Delicious. I must congratulate Henrietta on her cooking when she arrives.'

I decided to tell him the truth; see his reaction. 'She didn't make it. I did. Aunt Hetty' (I emphasised the

'Hetty') 'is useless at baking.' I swallowed a mouthful of my own tea, feeling it scald its way down to my stomach.

'Ha, ha,' he laughed nervously, uncertain whether to take me seriously or not, and flicked at an imaginary speck on his suit cuff. Before the situation could get any more awkward (and I wasn't sure if that was even possible) there was the sound of the front door opening and Aunt Hetty's regular call of 'Yoo hoo. I'm home!' The visitor jumped up, visibly startled into action and stood to attention behind the oak chair, smoothing down his already uncrumpled shirt. While he was sorting out his appearance, I took the opportunity to dart out of the room and down the stairs which Aunt Hetty was already beginning to ascend. She looked up at my approach and I noticed with alarm how tired and pale she was looking, like the ghost face from the night visit, not having seen her for more than a fleeting moment for a week. Aunt Hetty seemed a changed person from two weeks ago.

'Aunt Hetty!' I hissed urgently. 'There's a man in the kitchen. He says he's a friend but there's something funny about him.'

She stopped halfway up. 'What's his name?' she whispered back, and I suddenly realised that I had no idea what he was called.

'I don't know, I forgot to ask.' Aunt Hetty frowned and opened her mouth as if to reprimand me for forgetting my manners, so I quickly added, 'and he called you Henrietta.'

Her frown darkened, but she followed me up the stairs and into the kitchen without saying anything further. As we walked in, the man stepped forwards, extending his hand.

'Henrietta. Lovely to see you.'

I noticed he didn't say 'again'. Still bemused, Aunt Hetty shook his hand as I looked on. This was certainly not the behaviour of an old friend.

Seeing she was puzzled, the man said 'Dr Gallows. Nice of you to invite me.' Now I knew that was a lie, but Aunt Hetty seemed incapable of protesting.

'I've just come to tell you, "twenty-four hours".' Unbelievably, Aunt Hetty's face got even paler as she took a step backwards. He picked up his briefcase that was perched by his feet, and strode confidently towards the door.

'Twenty-four hours?' Aunt Hetty's usually strong and confident voice had a definite quaver to it.

'You've got twenty-four hours. That's all I can tell you.' He paused in the doorway. 'You know the rest.'

'Show him out please, Maisie,' Aunt Hetty murmured nodding her head downstairs.

I led Dr Gallows down to the front door. He paused at the mirror that hung by the coat hooks, inspecting his slickly gelled hair and tweaking an eyebrow carefully into place. I held the door open and waited.

'Farewell Maisie. Make sure your aunt remembers my visit.' He flashed his fake, blank-eyed smile, turned and walked smartly down the drive. I watched him and waited until he turned the corner and vanished from sight. Only then did I shut the door firmly, sliding the security chain and pulling it tightly across. I heard the clatter of pans in the kitchen, and ventured upstairs to confront Aunt Hetty.

Before I could even get a word out, she spoke, the fierceness in her voice surprising me considering how wretched she had sounded just a few moments earlier.

'How many times have I told you, never, never to invite strangers into the house when I'm not here?'

'Aunt Hetty, you saw what he was like. I tried to keep him out but he said he knew you, so he wasn't a stranger. It wasn't my fault,' I replied to her just as fiercely.

Her shoulders sagged into her sad shape, and I knew that she wasn't really cross.

'Okay. Don't worry, I believe you. And before you ask, Maisie, he was talking about work. A deadline.'

'But I thought he was a friend?' I asked, unsatisfied with her explanation.

'Work, friend, both. Now, no more questions Maisie, please!'

'But...'

'I mean it!' She slammed the dirty mugs into the sink and began rinsing them under the violently running tap. 'I have more work to do tonight and tomorrow so can you please cook and leave some out for me. If you're tired you can order a Chinese takeaway, or pizza or something, but I mustn't be disturbed. I've got to finish this project.'

I slumped onto a chair. Aunt Hetty was tired, I was tired and confused, and everything felt too much. I think Aunt Hetty sensed my feelings of dejection, because she came over to me. She checked, and then gave me a big, long hug. Suddenly I felt loved, contented and a little more able to take on the world again, the arms around me making me safe from outside things. But then she left, and I was alone. The pleasure I had felt at completing my art work had vanished and I wouldn't even have the satisfaction of being able to take her to see it tomorrow. I sighed again, but collected my thoughts and chose to focus on stopping the rumbling in my stomach. That was one problem I could tackle.

My arms ached from my day's painting, so I decided to take the easy option and order in a pizza, making sure the toppings were suitable for Aunt Hetty as well as me – black olives, mushrooms, spicy chicken, onions and sweetcorn. While I waited for the delivery I ran myself a bath, knowing the longer I left the paint splashes on my arms and face the harder they would be to remove. Besides that, I was just generally hot and sticky like a piece of melty bubble gum, and I wanted to cool down and feel smooth again. Lying under the bubbles, the water beginning to turn a slightly murky grey from the paint, a wind-up turtle paddled around me. Yellow rubber ducks could only bob listlessly by my toes, but this turtle was a brilliant swimmer and could also squirt water from his mouth – useful for targeting moths on dusky evenings. I stared up at the ceiling. I was fed up with being confused. I'd rather be back in a busy old market place surrounded by donkeys, men shouting and smelling of garlic, and birds in cages beakily squawking than here. Everything seemed so odd: not just one, or two, but three strangers turning up at the house; odd messages coming on paper, and arriving by person; friends and work colleagues who were obviously nothing of the sort...my brain suddenly stopped and thought only about that one word, work. That must be it, Aunt Hetty's work! Her projects were all quite important and occasionally even top secret. I thought back to a spy book I had read in the library. In that, a company tried to steal some of their rival's details about their latest project. It seemed to involve lots of different people threatening and warning others, and those other people running around being confused and then understanding and then being confused again and finally ending up that the most confused person was actually the one organising the theft in the first place. That could be what was happening here. I knew that some contracts ran into millions, if not billions, of pounds and the rivalry for business was tough and nasty. Aunt Hetty had told me that the company had been threatened by others before, most recently when they were working on a gel designed to create excess facial and body hair for men who wanted bushier beards and chests. Personally, I couldn't see the appeal of such of a product, but Aunt Hetty said that it was worth an awful lot of money and blackmailing letters had been sent to everyone in the company. Puce coloured paint had even been put over the director's very expensive black Bentley. I thought that would make a boring coloured car more exciting, but I understood that it wasn't really very nice. The perpetrators were caught before they could do anything else and I don't know what happened next.

Aunt Hetty hadn't told me what the latest project she was working on was exactly, apart from the titbit about dyed food. That meant it must be highly top secret, possibly even government-cloaked. The only problem was that I seemed to be the most confused person in this story, but I knew I wasn't the one organising everything, so I had no idea how the ending would go this time.

I huffed with the complexity of it all, wafting bubbles that had been wavering near my mouth down to the end of the bath, covering the turtle who had stopped his paddling and was now floating lazily by the plug chain. If what my brain had worked out was the real solution, then it was a big relief. It meant that even if Aunt Hetty was threatened, her company would look after her, and if the government were involved they would also give her assistance and protection. It still wasn't nice to think of men mysteriously running around in cloaks, suits, and dark cars, but at least Aunt Hetty wasn't alone. It also explained why she hadn't talked it through with me – she must have been forbidden under the Official Secrets Act or something like that. I do think it's funny that the Official Secrets Act isn't a secret as well; sometimes things are described by words that they're not. It's no wonder I can't make any sense of things at times.

I was very pleased with myself for working out the reasons for the recent goings-on. Although it upset me that Aunt Hetty was stressed and tired and too overworked even to properly talk with me, I sat down to eat my pizza that night feeling lighter and more relieved. It was as if the weight of confusion that had been heaped on my head had been lifted away. I ate my slices of pizza in the living room, sitting on the floor with the daily paper spread around me, reading everything I could about the news from foreign countries. Having been to so many places myself, the news from there was more real and reassuring than the local news somehow. I love pizza but I don't often eat it because Aunt Hetty taught me that the way I like to eat it isn't really okay to do when I'm in a restaurant. Some other people find it a bit odd (even disgusting) but I do it in the only way that makes sense to me. I cut it into slices and then I eat one slice at a time, but I eat the toppings off it one at a time in a particular order as well. I usually start with the biggest topping (like tomato slices or mushrooms) and end up with the sweetcorn or olives. Then I'll eat the base on its own. I don't mind some foods mixed together like in Bolognese or curry, but not on pizza. Aunt Hetty asked me why, and I couldn't answer. I don't know why; I just have to do it like I do or it tastes all wrong. Tonight there was no one in the room but me, so I could eat as I needed to without thinking of anyone else. I licked the last cheesy strands from my fingers, finished reading the cartoons on the back page of the paper, and went off to rinse my greasy hands in the kitchen.

I'd left half of the pizza on a plate under foil for Aunt Hetty to eat when she wanted later. Drying my hands, I picked up the cardboard box our meal had arrived in and took it downstairs and out into the back garden to the recycling dustbin. However much Aunt Hetty likes old-fashioned contraptions and designs within the house, she's very much up to date in her thoughts about recycling and 'making the world a greener place' as she says. It's all logical to me and I like having lots of bins to sort things into. Opening the lid of the paper bin I was about to stuff the box in when the contents caught my eye. Brown paper. Parcel paper all screwed up. I lifted out the top ball and found three more underneath. Parcels? I hadn't known Aunt Hetty to receive any parcels other than from my mum and dad, and she always told me about them. She never usually ordered anything that would need delivering, and all of her friends lived close by. Intrigued, I quickly gathered the paper under my arm, put the pizza box where it belonged and clanged on the bin lid.

Once inside, I returned to the living room, and cleared the newspapers off the floorboards. In their place, I spread out the brown parcel paper, smoothing it as flat as its crinkly surface would allow. I sat back and studied them. The first thing I noticed was that they were not (as I had secretly hoped) from my parents. Although Aunt Hetty's not telling me about any correspondence from them would have been almost unforgivable, I knew it would have been for a good reason, and at least there would have been contact of sorts, even if it wasn't personal to me. But the handwriting of the addresses was neither my mum's perfect italic calligraphic lettering nor Dad's practically illegible scrawl. Instead, it was simply neatly printed letters that slanted gently towards the right and had a little curl on the ends of the letters with long ends such as P and Y − perfect for the postman to read, but nearly impossible to distinguish from the handwriting of thousands of other people. I wondered if I examined the letters more that I might be able to, but I didn't have anything to compare them to at the moment, so it really wasn't of much use. Still, even if the writing wasn't exciting, the stamps and postmarks might reveal more about the sender.

I inspected them closely. The stamps gave no clues, for they were all sent from the United Kingdom. But the postmarks revealed that they were from four different locations: London, Caerdydd, Truro and Penzance. By the looks of things, they were sent only a few days apart, and by the same person, meaning that someone had been travelling fairly quickly around the country. The parcels must have been tied up with string because there was no sticky tape attached, which was lucky because it meant that the paper had not been ripped in the need to open them. I realised they had all arrived in the past two weeks otherwise they would have been thrown out when the dustmen collected the rubbish last Monday morning. I examined the sizes of the paper – large, very large, smallish and tiny. So, even though it was the same person sending the packages, they didn't contain the same amount of things each time. I had no idea who could possibly have sent them. Of course, I'd come into contact with lots of people during my travels with my parents, but they weren't in the habit of writing to me, let alone Aunt Hetty, and most of them were still far away in foreign places. As far as I knew, Aunt Hetty didn't have any close acquaintances in any of these places, but for someone to send four packages so close together they must have been fairly well known to her.

I turned the papers over, around and around, but there were no other distinguishing marks that I could see. And then suddenly, in minuscule writing made by the same hand as the addressee, I saw a short line of words written along one of the folds in the smallest rectangle of package paper, the one that had arrived first. It was so small; I had to squeeze my eyes really tight, squinting to decipher the letters. 'COPY AND KEEP. PASS ON TO M WHEN CAN. STAY SAFE.'

Copy and keep what? It could only mean the contents of the parcel, and I had no idea what that was. And 'M'? Was that me? It could be, but it could also mean Marcus, Aunt Hetty's architect friend. Or Marguerite, the eccentric, old and crabbedy lady who lived next door with her two chihuahuas (although this seemed unlikely). Or Meena, one of Aunt Hetty's closest work colleagues and friends – a scientist who specialised in some strange branch of genetics. This was silly. Here I was, sitting on the floor of the living room at ten o'clock at night, trying to analyse rubbish. I could have just been playing a trivial game, but I couldn't stop my brain ticking over, trying to make things clearer.

It must be Meena, I decided, reasoning that the parcels would need to be work related for Aunt Hetty to have kept their arrival quiet. Questions went round and round the inside of my head with this mediocre solution I had conjured up. Questions such as why had they been sent here and not to work? And why hadn't they been sent to Meena directly? I didn't have any answers and I was getting an ache across the front of my face as I tried to concentrate on everything so I decided my time as a super-sleuth must come to an end. I simply didn't have the skills (or the clues) to work out anything further. The most sensible thing I could do was to go to bed.

I remember this now and I laugh. I thought it could have ended there, the mystery subsiding, leaving my brain free to think about other things. But in reality, while I thought my detective work had been brought to an unsatisfactory conclusion, it was only just beginning.

CHAPTER

7

I woke late the next morning, looking with surprise at the hands pointing to nine-fourteen on my watch lying on my bedside table, the sun streaming through a crack in the curtains. I usually woke early, finding it hard to sleep once the sun had risen, but today I had obviously been tired enough to sleep through the lightening of day from night. When it's light, my brain tells me to get up, and I have to train myself to remember that seeing the sun doesn't always equal daytime. Two years ago we were tracking some reindeer herds in the north of Norway. Up in the mountains, the sun didn't go down at all. And my brain didn't stop working either. I could run around chasing trolls and hunting cloudberries all day everyday, and it was only because my parents spent some time training me to stop, wind down and go to sleep, that I managed to get any rest at all.

My insides had the feeling of being hungry. It's as if my stomach is a blow-up ball getting slowly squeezed and deflating. All twisty and small. So I jumped out of bed, did the underwear, socks, shorts and T-shirt routine, and went in search of some food. As I walked into the kitchen I stopped – Aunt Hetty was sitting at the table, paper in hand, glass of orange juice to the side. She looked up at me.

'Morning, sleepyhead Maisie! Have a nice rest?'

I nodded my head in reply as she continued.

'I felt so bad about leaving you all alone this week I decided to cancel my work for today and spend it with you instead. I want to come and see what you've been making at Dina's, and then I thought we could go for a walk in the park, feed the ducks, and eat ice-creams.'

I'd never done this kind of thing when I was little and I loved it now. I had been more used to feeding parrots and monkeys. So I loved to watch the ducks, safe in the knowledge that there were no piranhas or crocodiles to suddenly pull them under the murky water.

'Oh, yes!' The day was looking much brighter. Although it was a change to what I thought was happening, it was a good change. 'That would be great, Aunt Hetty! I can't wait to show you my totem pole.'

It was so unusual for her to postpone work, even on a weekend, yet she did look tired with panda circles under her eyes – I wondered if she'd decided that even she needed to take a break before becoming completely exhausted.

And so that was our plans sorted, now I just needed to eat and we could go. I poured out some cornflakes in a bowl, spooned honey on the top and started crunching. I don't like milk on cereal, it makes it stick to my tongue and I can't swallow. And honey is one of the best things ever. Nearly anything is made better if it has honey on it (apart from mashed potato, that didn't work at all). When I taste honey, it's as though a zillion bees are whizzing to the back of my head, buzzing around and behind my eyes. It makes me want to open my eyes really, really wide. It's a bee party in my brain.

The rest of the day went brilliantly. Although Aunt Hetty was quiet on the walk over to Dina's, when we got there she started talking and her face became pink and warm as I showed her my work as well as Dina's creations. By the time we'd stopped off for sandwiches and bread for the ducks she seemed her normal bubbly self. Fizzy drink bubbles make my mouth have fireworks. Aunt Hetty's bubbles make me feel fireworks inside. We fed the ducks, swans and hissy geese a whole loaf of brown farmhouse, but they still seemed hungry so I gave a particularly bedraggled-looking white duck the end of my ice-cream cone. This didn't impress the big swans who wanted more, but I ignored them, watching the birds peck and squabble at the small torn pieces of soggy bread floating on the surface of the lake. We eventually left them to their own devices and walked the scenic route home along the bank of the river. Once there, we cooked, ate and washed up together before settling down to watch one of our favourite films. For the whole day we had managed to keep up nearly continuous conversation without once mentioning anything to do with Aunt Hetty's work. I had at least expected a brief update, but even that was not forthcoming. So I concentrated on simply enjoying spending some proper time with her again.

Once the credits of *My Family and Other Animals* began rolling, and I got up to go to bed, she said, 'Doing anything interesting tomorrow, Maisie?'

I sighed. 'School project. I thought I might do something on totem poles and Native Americans seeing as that's all I've been thinking about this week.'

'Good, excellent,' she murmured. She didn't seem to be listening to me and was staring through the window at the sky which was a startling shade of sunset red. 'Just, you know, I'll be back at work and I want you to keep busy. Not spend all your time on your own here...' she trailed off, before carrying on in a half-jokey tone like her voice was bouncing up and down, 'and I don't want to find any strangers in the kitchen when I get home, thank you!' She turned and grinned. I grinned back, but knew that she was being serious.

'No worries! Are you off early in the morning?'

'No. I want to work from home first thing, but I'll be out in the afternoon. It might be best if you go to the library in the morning, so the house is completely quiet.'

'All right.' I agreed. 'But it's not as if I'm exactly the noisiest person.' I considered myself to be fairly quiet – I don't play music loudly, and only occasionally hummed or sang as I wandered around.

'True. But those elephant feet of yours on the stairs are enough to distract anyone.'

I had to admit she had a point; I did tend to run, leap or jump around on the flight of stairs. Walking up or down them just seemed so boring. My longest leap up was six steps, and down I had progressed to twelve and was determined to beat it. It looked like tomorrow morning wouldn't be the time to break the record, however.

'Night, then.'

'Goodnight. See you tomorrow evening.'

I left, leaving her to her own devices which probably involved reading another chapter of a thick Russian novel that just read 'dull dull dull' to me, and then heading downstairs to bed.

By the time I'd eaten breakfast the next day, the rain had begun to come down, drizzling slightly at first, and then settling into a steady downpour that looked to set in for the day. As Aunt Hetty had predicted, there was no sign of her, but because her scooter was in its parking place I knew she was still in the house. I don't like rain. It gets in everywhere and makes you prickle. Frustrated with Aunt Hetty at asking me to leave the house, despite the rain, I deliberately clumped noisily up to my bedroom to get my bag and raincoat. By the time I had finished dressing, covering up as much as I could to avoid getting wet, I was bit sorry I'd been cross, so made the journey downstairs as quietly as possible. There was an umbrella stand by the door, but it was a liar, as it never had any umbrellas in it. Although I searched for one in the jumble of dusters, carrier bags, old shoes and cobwebs that was called the 'cupboard under the stairs', there was no sign of an umbrella anywhere.

'Typical,' I thought, doing up my top button, practically strangling myself and tying the toggles of my hood tightly together. With no umbrella, my satchel would get wet, but I would have to hope that its contents of notebook, pencils and indispensable town map would stay dry.

Despite the sky's appearance of being able to rain all day, as I reached the library, the downpour had slowed to an occasional fat drip, and I felt thoroughly overdressed. I was sticky under my waterproofs, as it was warm despite the clouds. Weather doesn't make sense here. In lots of hot countries it's really, really warm in the day and the sun is out. Then it's night, and it's dark, and it's cold. You know what to expect and when. Here, you get sunny days in the snow, and cloudy days that are really warm. I never know what to wear. I left my wet clothes in the library's lobby, along with many other people's, and made my way up to the second-floor study area.

'Morning, Maisie!' Mr Jabber, a retired butterfly specialist, looked up from his regular seat in the corner of the reference section. He was nearly always in the library when I was there, and we enjoyed chatting together during reading breaks about the different countries we had both visited. I could see several huge tomes spread around him this morning, so decided not to go over. Instead I waved, and went to look for some books of my own.

Sitting by a window, I began to flick through pages, looking at numerous totem pole designs. Before too long I was engrossed by the pictures and words, and began furiously writing down information into my notebook. It was Mr Jabber accidentally dropping an animal encyclopaedia (letters Za–Zu) on the floor that made me suddenly look up. He smiled at me and mouthed 'sorry', and quickly slotted it back into place on the shelf. I checked my watch – one-thirty-seven! I decided that I'd done enough at the library for today. Checking two large books out at the front desk, I had already begun to re-dress myself in raincoat and boots before realising that the rain had properly stopped and there was a bit of sun in between the clouds. Half-pleased, and half-irritated at the ability of English weather to change so abruptly, I took my coat off and slung it over my arm before beginning my walk home. As I walked, dodging the biggest of the puddles but splashing through the smaller ones, the sky grew clearer and clearer.

I planned my afternoon in my head. I like to know what I'm doing so that I can look forward to doing it. I also don't like it if I forget to do something I need to, so planning helps a lot. I would have a toasted sandwich in the kitchen and then, so long as the sun remained, I would go out into the garden to do some excavating.

Aunt Hetty's garden had once had a rubbish dump at the bottom of the grounds, and she'd given me permission to dig for old bottles, pottery and miscellaneous metal artefacts 'to my hearts content'. I wasn't sure exactly what that was, but when I was digging, I felt like I was exploring, which connected me to my parents. And that made me feel calm and happy inside. So perhaps that was what she meant. I'd so far uncovered over 150 remnants and there was still plenty of ground left to dig. There was nothing hugely valuable, but I was gathering a great collection of assorted glass bottles, shards of pottery and a few weird, twisty metal mysteries. I was still hoping to find a glass bottle that was complete with stopper, maybe even one with a weird potion still inside!

Once I'd done some digging, it would probably be time to start cooking (or at least preparing) the evening meal. But what to make tonight? I was pondering through the options when I turned the corner into Halfway Street – the road which Aunt Hetty's house is on. Her house is the sixth one on the left, which is why I could immediately see the car parked outside her gate. There were no others, everyone was at work, so the back of the big black Land Rover was clearly in view, as was the horrifying sight of someone being pushed headfirst through the car's back door. Two dark-suited and closely shaven men were holding the person's hands behind their back and were gagging their mouth. I didn't know what to do. My legs stopped walking and I was still as an ice statue, and then suddenly my insides became ice as well – it wasn't just anyone being forced into the car, it was Aunt Hetty! I knew it was her from the clothes, the hair and then the face as it twisted around to stare straight at me before the door was finally slammed on her struggling body. The two men didn't even look around, they just leapt into the front of the car and accelerated quickly away down the street. Although I'd been frozen, my legs suddenly thawed and I began to run. When I reached the front gate, though, I realised the futility of it. I didn't have a hope of catching the vehicle on foot, and even if I could quickly find someone to drive me, I had no idea where the car was heading. The car had left tyre marks on the tarmac as it sped away and they were the only sign that anything at all had just happened. If they hadn't been there, I would have doubted the events that had just taken place before my very eyes. My aunt, Hetty Voyager, had just been kidnapped! And I, Maisie Voyager, had no idea what to do.

CHAPTER

It may seem surprising to you, but calling the police wasn't something I wanted to do. Moving from place to place, my parents had to rely on themselves or the people they were with if they needed help. When we were in the Himalayas, and two of the guides disappeared overnight with some donkeys and a week's worth of food, we just got on with it. There was no one to call and no one you could report the theft to. So the idea of relying on the police was new to me. And I was also worried that if I called, they'd come in cars with sirens wailing and screaming. I hate sirens. It's someone sticking a pin into you but with a sound. Or like sucking a lemon with your ears and you just want to curl up into a ball and hide. If I hear them when I'm out, I have to put my hands on my ears, or hide in a hood, or stick my head under Aunt Hetty's coat. Which I know other people don't do but I'd rather do that than feel ill. So police sirens were the last thing I wanted. And there was another reason: I just didn't think they would believe me – everything sounded too unbelievable to be true, a story. I remembered from adventure books that if they did start to believe me, this could put Aunt Hetty's life in even more danger. And, going to the police meant having to speak to strangers, explain myself, and what would happen to me then? They wouldn't know me, might not understand what I was saying. And then I might be forced to live somewhere else, perhaps forever. I couldn't cope with that. It would be all wrong. I felt my breathing start to go in in in in in again and forced myself to breathe out so my chest would loosen.

Maybe, I thought to myself, I would go to the police later on if I absolutely had to, but for now I wanted a chance to think things through on my own.

I bit my lip hard as I walked up the drive and saw the front door ajar. Aunt Hetty hadn't even been given the chance to close it. Entering the house, I felt my eyes watering. I don't often cry and I don't usually know when I'm going to or why I'm doing it. I get worried it's my thoughts leaking out of me, and other people will be able to tell what's going on in my head. But I knew these tears were because I was scared for Aunt Hetty, and had to bite my lip hard to stop the tears from running down my cheeks. I gritted my teeth and willed them to stay in my eyes. However bad I felt, it wouldn't help Aunt Hetty. If all I could do was cry and feel lonely, I might as well go to the police station right now and give up on everything. My Voyager stubbornness kicked in (a notorious family trait) and I decided to get organised. The first thing to do would be to go through every piece of information I had in the aim of finding some clue as to what was going on, and where Aunt Hetty might have been taken. I climbed the flights of stairs to my room, sat at my desk overlooking the front garden, in view of the street (and any potential unwelcome visitors) and got out my notebook. I didn't think that the kidnappers had spotted me when they were bundling Aunt Hetty inside their car, but I wanted to make sure I was able to see if anyone approached the house.

I made a list of all of the information I had so far, in numerical (and timed) order, just as I thought a detective would. Next to the points, in a red pen, I wrote questions and marked things that I wanted to find out more about:

1. 7:30 p.m. (approximately), Tuesday 11th July

    - Dark-cloaked visitor came to see Aunt Hetty. Met in study.

    - Came in silver car – old-fashioned, don't know what type but there was a bird or flying thing on the front sticking up. The end letters of the number plate were FIG.

- Driver = male, big black beard, long dark hair. Dark glasses. Shiny, silver-coloured ring worn on right hand.

2. 7:15 p.m. (approx.), Friday 14th July

   - Silver car from before seen in Tango Street, opposite Clare's Coffee Shop.

   - Same driver. Car pulled up at kerb briefly and then drove off again, heading west. *Could this be a coincidence?*

3. 8:45 p.m. (approx.), Friday 14th July

   - Note placed on meal table by unknown person(s) at Spirrelli Pirrelli's Italian Restaurant. Note written in black capital letters by thick felt-tip pen.

     > AN ANORAK HAS ONE; THERE ARE TWO IN A KNOCK,
     >
     > THE NEXT IS IN TOY BUT NOT IN A TOCK,
     >
     > THE THIRD IS IN NEWT, A WARNING AND PLAN,
     >
     > AND ALSO IN UNDERSTAND THIS IF YOU CAN.
     >
     > THE FOURTH CAN BE CAUGHT IN THE MIDDLE OF CAT
     >
     > AND IN A FAT RAT WHO'S WEARING A HAT.
     >
     > THE FIFTH IS IN NUT, AND ONCE FOUND IN NEWS,
     >
     > THE SIXTH IS IN CHALLENGE AND THE BEGINNING OF CLUES.

THE LAST CAN BE FOUND AT THE END OF THIS
NOTE, AND ALSO THE LAST OF THE LETTERS I
WROTE.

NOT UP IN THE MOUNTAINS, BUT DOWN BY THE
SEA,

IS WHERE YOU WILL FIND THEM - G, M AND P.

4. 12:32 a.m., Saturday 15th July

- Dark-cloaked stranger seen in Aunt Hetty's study.

- Stranger took away all papers from Aunt Hetty's wooden chest. *What did the papers say?*

- Aunt Hetty given a warning about safety. Her face was a ghost mask, she was scared. *Why?*

5. 7:04 p.m. (approx.), Saturday 22nd July

- A visitor in a smart suit called Dr Gallows. Fishy eyes.

- He said he knew Aunt Hetty but obviously wasn't a close friend. *Why did he lie?*

- Told Aunt Hetty she had 'twenty-four hours'. *Twenty-four hours before what?*

6. Saturday 22nd July

- Papers found in dustbin.

- Came from London, Caerdydd, Truro and Penzance. Sent on 7th, 11th, 14th and 16th of July. The second was sent on the same day as visitor came to see Aunt Hetty. *Could there be a link?*

- Message inside read 'COPY AND KEEP. PASS ON TO M WHEN CAN. STAY SAFE.'

7. 2:04 p.m., Monday 24th July

- Aunt Hetty kidnapped by two bald men.

- Put into black Land Rover, it had muddy wheels and black windows. Can't remember registration number. Drove off down Halfway Street away from the town centre.

- Front door to house left unlocked.

I looked at my list; there were seven points. Frowning, I tried to recall if there was anything else I should add. Maybe Aunt Hetty's mood and behaviour? Not sure if it was a valid enough clue to warrant a number, I simply added at the bottom *Aunt Hetty acting strange – getting irritated with me, very tired and mostly uncommunicative.* The problem was I hadn't really seen enough of her, especially over the last seven days, to note down anything more detailed.

I re-read the list over and over and over again, trying to make some connections and find something of use, when one thing jumped out at me. Twenty-four hours! What was it Dr Gallows had said? 'You've got twenty-four hours.' That was on Saturday evening. And what if Aunt Hetty hadn't done whatever it was she was supposed to do by last night? Maybe Dr Gallows had kidnapped her? I got excited for a moment, and then realised that he definitely wasn't one of the two men I had seen earlier unless he'd suddenly shaved his head. Remembering how much time he'd spent looking at himself in the mirror checking his hair was perfect, I didn't think this was likely. Back to the beginning…unless…unless…he was only part of this mystery. Perhaps he'd ordered her kidnap, or maybe he also worked for the person who had.

On a new sheet of paper I wrote 'Dr Gallows = kidnap?' at the top. It seemed a reasonable idea but it didn't help me much. After staring at the paper for a few minutes, the words began wiggling and waving around, twisting into horrible shapes. They came up off the page as if they were trying to crawl into my eyes and head and take over my brain. I turned over the paper quickly; staring at my writing was not going to give me any help whatsoever. Leaving the desk, I flopped down on my bed, and then jumped straight off again, whipping my covers away at the same time. On my mattress was the source of the crinkly-rustling sound I had heard as I lay down. It was a piece of paper wonkily folded into four, the edges meeting unevenly. I opened it quickly, and smoothed it out onto my lap.

Dear Maisie,

I hope that you won't get this note; that I will be able to remove it before you ever have need to find it. But if you do, you will know that I am gone. I cannot explain much, because that would put you in danger too, and I do not want to risk that. I know this is hard, but I can't tell you when I may return. Wait for a parcel that will come today or tomorrow, it will give you more clues to help. When you have it, leave the house and find somewhere safer to stay.

I do not know where they are taking me, and if you are asked by anyone where I am, you must say that I have gone away with work. The safest thing would be for you to go to the police, but if you chose the harder path, stay as safe as you can Maisie. When the parcel comes, do what it says. There is some money underneath the beetle case in my study, take what you need – I hope it will be enough. Do not be scared, use your Voyager head and follow it wisely.

I will see you again, I just hope it will be soon.

With fond love,

Aunt Hetty

I had to re-read the letter several times before I could understand all of it. In reality, it told me nothing apart from the fact that I had to wait for a parcel. And that if I went to the police, it was safer for me, but it could also cause more problems. I thought for a while, holding the letter tightly in my hands. There were some creaks from the house walls, but I couldn't hear anything else. Not even cars from outside. While I thought, it was as though the rest of the world had disappeared. Then I decided: I would wait for the parcel, but I would also see if I could work out where Aunt Hetty had gone. There was no point otherwise. I wanted her to be safe as well as me. I didn't feel safe unless she was. It wasn't like I could just go back to my parents; I had no idea even where they were at the moment. It probably would have involved a plane ride, possible helicopter survey of the desert (or jungle) terrain, and then a camel, canoe or yak ride lasting anything from an hour to several days long. Even then, the only chance I might have of tracking them down would be the possible sighting of some makeshift tents, the hastily stamped out remains of a three-day-old cooking fire, or the scuffed footprint of a European man-made boot. Hardly likely. It was usually difficult enough for the local people to track my parents down, let alone me. I had eleven years experience of their habits, but too many of those years didn't count considering I'd been papoose-bound to my mum's back.

No, tracking my parents down simply involved too much headwork to consider, as much as I wanted to. I loved Aunt Hetty, and although I'd found living with her difficult to get used to, I now felt comfortable with her. But part of me had always longed to be back with my mum and dad learning how to trap the Greater Moroccan Blue-Tongued Moth, or being taught how to avoid being caught by the Sasquatch in Nepal. I shook my head fiercely. It was no use thinking down these lines, not when Aunt Hetty was being held who knows where. I had to focus on her, but where to start? I sat on my bed, clutching her letter, staring at the list on my desk. Pausing, wondering. I was sort of scared, but sort of okay. Although there was a lot about the situation that I didn't know, that I didn't understand, I could also start to find some logic in it. This was a puzzle that needed to be fixed, similar to the crosswords I liked. I just had to think about the clues and where they led, and not focus on what might happen if I couldn't find the answers. Only, I wasn't too sure my usual crossword trick would work here – I couldn't just fit my own solutions to the problems, I had to actually work them out.

Suddenly the doorbell rang. It made me jump as I wasn't expecting it. I know what the doorbell is for, but I wish I lived in a super science-fiction house with a TV screen showing the person's face instead. Or back in a hut made from bamboo and palm leaves – they had enough space in the walls that you could always see anyone (or anything) coming. So from the bell I knew someone was at the door, but not who, and that bothered me more than anything. I leapt off my bed, and jumped across to the window, peering down to the front of the house. However, the perpetrator had stepped into the porch, and I couldn't see who had rung the bell. I hesitated, unsure what to do, remembering Aunt Hetty's warning about avoiding strangers. Then two small rats on leads came into view. Marguerite's chihuahuas! They were not my favourite creatures in the world, and dogs didn't really compare to lemurs and lizards, but at least they were less harmful than some of the recent visitors to the house. I wasn't too keen on Marguerite though. She was a fake lady in the same way Dr Gallows was fake. Marguerite was all smiles, swooshy skirts, perfume and perfect clothes. But then saying things she didn't mean and making you feel like she was squashing you flat as a dead flea. I didn't think she really liked anyone else very much at all. Then the bell rang a second time, more insistently, so I capered down the stairs, skidded to a halt on the front door mat, and opened the door.

'Ah! Maisie! Hetty not in?' Marguerite Hibble peered around me, as if Aunt Hetty was lurking in the background.

'No. Sorry Miss Hibble. She's…' I came to an abrupt halt. What should I say? What could I tell people? I couldn't remember Aunt Hetty's words in the letter. I expected if I told Marguerite the truth, she would overreact, collapse into a faint and upon recovering would go into shrieking hysterics about my safety, and demand to call the police.

'She's what, child?' Marguerite demanded. She looked directly at me.

It was as if her eyes were peering into my head and could see all of my thoughts tripping over each other. As a rule, I don't look at people, I look to the side. It doesn't hurt as much. I shifted my eyes away and looked down. Trixie and Mixie were lurking near my ankles, and I took a step back, away from nipping teeth. I took a deep breath and composed myself, and finally remembered what to say, 'She's working on a big project – she's hardly here at the moment. In and out, in and out...can I help you at all?' I remembered to ask the helpful bit at the end.

Marguerite frowned. She wasn't used to having her plans inconvenienced by such matters as people not being there when she wanted them.

'I just wanted to give her this.' She burrowed in her carpet bag, displacing three lace handkerchiefs with curly pink M's on the corners, two bus tickets and six assorted dog biscuits (bone-shaped) before emerging triumphantly with a brown envelope. 'It came through my door by mistake this morning. The postman must have put it through with *Chihuahua's Weekly*. Will you make sure she gets it – the flap's come unstuck a little, I'm afraid.'

The letter looked like it was about to fall apart, covered in numerous rips, tears and smears. Marguerite handed it over, and on closer inspection, I saw it must have been the victim of Trixie's (or Mixie's) over-enthusiastic attentions.

'Thank you,' I said, knowing I should be polite even though it was a bit rude of her not to apologise for the damage. 'Aunt Hetty will appreciate it.'

'That's quite all right, I do like to be of service. Goodbye then, Maisie, you must come round and play with Trixie and Mixie soon, they'd love a little playmate!'

I growled inside but continued smiling at her as she started down the drive. I was just about to shut the door when she turned.

'Oh, and Maisie? Would you please ask Hetty if she could keep her late-night visitors to a minimum? Most disturbing when one is trying to get some beauty sleep. Goodbye!'

CHAPTER 9

I shut the door hard in my cross way, thinking that Aunt Hetty was lucky to have been taken away if it meant she didn't have to deal with Marguerite Hibble, but then I re-thought – maybe not. I looked at the letter in my hand, half expecting it to be the parcel Aunt Hetty had told me would arrive, but it was simply the boring telephone bill. Completely unexciting and not in the least bit helpful in my investigations. Things were no clearer now than they were five minutes ago.

I aimlessly wandered upstairs, not certain what to do with myself, wishing I had something to keep me company. Perhaps a dog would be okay. Not a ratty, nippy thing like Trixie or Mixie but a proper dog that would bark, not squeak, and sit at your feet rather than on them. In the kitchen, I felt hungry. Food is one of the things that makes me know where I am in the day. It keeps a routine, helps me to break the day up. And it's like my own personal hug to myself. If you have an empty tummy you feel like a hollow tree. And if you have a full tummy, you're suddenly alive and growing and can do anything! Although I was going to have to wait around for a parcel (I still wasn't certain how I was going to fill up my time), I knew that once it arrived things would start to happen. I made a mug of coffee and sat at the table, trying to decide what to do. I stared at the surface, watching patterns form and swirl in the liquid. The dark and light brown twisted and swam around. There was nothing but me and the mug. I let my head go completely into what I could see, everything else in the world was shut out and I felt a bit safer again. Then I turned my head and suddenly came back to earth. There was a long dark swirl that looked like Chile, another like the coast of Ireland, and a little one was... I sat upright. Countries! Places! Running up to my room, I grabbed a scrap of paper, and was soon in the kitchen absorbing everything I could from the riddle from the restaurant. Mountains, sea...if I could work out the puzzle, then maybe the word would be a place? I wasn't sure who, or what 'G, M and P' were, but it seemed more important to try and work out the most complicated bit first.

I chewed on the end of my pencil, studying the words. Anorak and knock, that must be 'K'. The next one was

'Y', then 'N', followed by 'A' and then another 'N', 'C' and finally an 'E' – KYNANCE. I looked at the word I'd written at the bottom, 'KYNANCE'. The name meant nothing to me. I wasn't even sure if it was a country or place. I sighed. Bother, it was all getting so complicated, and it looked like I'd have to make another trip to the library to see if I could find where the word came from.

'Maisie you fool,' I told myself off. Aunt Hetty had numerous books covering anything and everything and until recently she had owned a fat volume which contained maps of every country in the world. One afternoon I was reading *Swallows and Amazons* and decided to make my own boat. Not for me to sail in (I didn't have that much time or skill), but a boat big enough for a toy sailor. I fashioned a raft out of bottles and used a long ruler for a mast. I tried it out in the bath but it kept tipping over to one side. It needed ballast, weight to even it out. I needed something that would keep her floating steady. I tried several different things until I came to the book. And it worked! My boat floated steady! Now that I had made a successful ship I wanted to see where else she could sail. So off I went to the lake. I pushed her away from the edge and away she merrily glided. I clapped my hands in pleasure. Then a stupid white duck, bobbing for weed, came up to the surface, catching the edge of the boat…and up and over it went. And the map of the world sunk, Alaska and Africa settling on the sediment at the bottom.

'Bother, bother, bother.' I said it a lot, all the way home. It didn't really describe my frustration. I was more bothered about my boat than the book, but I knew Aunt Hetty would be more bothered about the book than the boat and I didn't want to get told off. Luckily Aunt Hetty generously understood so I didn't feel too guilty. However, now that little escapade meant that I had to go all the way to the library to look at an atlas, which was much more irritating.

'Get riddle, get riddle, get riddle.' I repeated it to myself over and over as I went down to the front door to pick up my satchel and coat. I had to make sure it was on my mental list of things to do, that I'd burnt the words into my mind. If I didn't, I'd forget and pootle all the way to the library before realising I'd left it back at home. As I opened the front door, a parcel flew through the air and landed with a flump on the front door mat. A bicycle courier whizzed off down the drive to the road.

'Oy!' I shouted, annoyed at being surprised but he just rang his bell in a jaunty farewell. I hoped that whatever was in the parcel wasn't broken, but when I picked it up, it was so light that I realised I needn't have worried. It didn't even feel like there was anything in there to break. I looked at my watch. The library was going to shut in two hours. I had to get there if I was going, so I decided to put the package in my bag and look at it when I was there. I checked to make sure it was the one I was expecting, rather than another random bill or useless package for Aunt Hetty containing some strange purchase such as fluffy walking socks or a CD of warbling opera singers. Yes, it was addressed to me –

Miss M. Voyager – the postmark was local, I noticed, and the handwriting different from Aunt Hetty's packages.

'Enough,' I told myself out loud, 'save it for later.'

An Encyclopaedia of the World and All Its Countries. I pulled the enormous book towards me, hefted a huge wodge of pages over until I reached the index and began running my finger down and down a list of place names. Nothing. No 'Kynance' mentioned anywhere. Not even under an obscure section about places that no longer existed. Maybe I was thinking too big. I put the book back onto the shelf, and took down the one next to it, *Cities and Towns of the United Kingdom.* This might be better. Again, I began searching the index Keele... Kilkenny...Kingston...and then yes! Kynance! Kynance Cove in Cornwall. I'd been to Cornwall once before with my parents, but it was when I was three, and all I could remember was charging around Tintagel Castle on a cliff top, pretending I was a knight of King Arthur while the sea crashed majestically below. I needed to find out all I could, so I turned to page 427 and began to read.

Fifty-seven minutes later I had become more accustomed to the landscape of Cornwall. I could tell you that the southernmost tip of England, Land's End, was there, that the Cornish language evolved during the Iron Age, that the Cornish word for 'dragon' was 'druic' and that once upon a time Cornwall had the highest number of tin mines in England. It was very interesting, but not particularly helpful. Still, I felt pleased I'd managed to work out the riddle, and that my initial suspicion that the word was a place name was correct. But I still didn't know what 'G, M and P' stood for. There were just too many questions and not enough answers…and then I remembered the parcel waiting for me in my bag; maybe that would provide some. I decided to inspect it as if I was a forensic scientist. I didn't have tweezers and a microscope, but if I squeezed my eyes up small and peered through a tiny gap in my closed fist, things sort of looked bigger. And I could use my thumb and forefinger to pick up tiny things, so perhaps I was a scientist in the making.

I examined the outside first. No interesting marks; it was posted yesterday by someone who could print letters in minuscule, yet legible writing. The letters were weeny, about half a centimetre high and with triangles and squares. They weren't round and bubbly shapes. It was like calculator writing, all sort of digital. Carefully I unstuck the top of the parcel and peered inside. I sniffed first, as I remembered that if you did this, you might get extra clues. But I couldn't smell anything apart from glue and that weird dead fishy smell of some paper. Inside there was a single piece of paper, and a small bundle of papers. I quickly pulled them out and put all of the things on to my lap, out of sight of any nearby readers and nosey librarians. The bundle of papers was pages and pages of densely inked notes. The words made no sense, and didn't even look like any language that existed. They weren't English letters or Arabic. It was more like hieroglyphics and random squiggles – squares, circles, dots and spirals. Some on their own, others looped and linked together. It could be an unknown language, or someone's own personal code, something that no one else could read but them. I turned some more pages, but could get no indication of what the notes were about at all. It was most peculiar. Intrigued (and a little excited) I looked at the single sheet of paper, it was a letter, and I hoped all would be explained. The writing was the same as the pointy one from the front of the parcel paper.

Dear Maisie,

If you get this then you will know that Hetty has been taken away. I will explain everything to you at a later point, but first I have to ask you to trust me. I can help you to find Hetty and protect the secrets she holds. Keep these papers safe next to you all of the time – we will need them later on.

Meet me at St Tinto's church on Justible Street, in the graveyard by the old yew tree. Come with this bundle of papers, any other savings Hetty has left for you, and all of the clues and information you have hoarded so far. I will be at the church at ten o'clock on Monday night. I will wait for two hours but no more, or it will become too dangerous. Please be there.

When you have read this, remember what I've said, and then destroy it. It absolutely must not fall into the wrong hands.

I turned the page around, trying to read the signature, but it stayed a squiggle whichever way up it was even if I looked at it through my hand microscope…and maybe that was the point? I thought about the content of the note, more than a little worried that it could all turn out to be a horrible trick, and I could end up being snatched, the same as Aunt Hetty. But then I remembered that Aunt Hetty herself had told me to wait for the package, meaning that she must know who sent it, and that they were not the enemy.

Ten o'clock at night was late. I wasn't allowed to go out after eight usually but it was summer, dusk didn't come until nine or so. If this person wanted to meet without being seen by many people, they needed to wait until dark. I'd have to brave the night and all it might contain.

My head was going like a roundabout with everything whizzing. I needed to make some order and the first thing I needed to do was to get rid of the note. Could I shred it? Not very easily here in the library, as I would most likely be reprimanded about making a mess by a bespectacled librarian. Suddenly, I remembered a trick I had once read about in another spy book (books and films did come in handy for teaching me new things). I screwed up the paper into the smallest ball possible, and put it into my mouth. My cheeks hamster-bulged as I tried to reduce the unappetising mass. It tasted like some really bad fish I'd once started eating in Costa Rica. I think the fish had been overcooked, but this just tasted bad because it was paper and not meant to be eaten.

I chewed, and chewed, and chewed. And gradually it began to get smaller. Still chomping, I packed up my stuff and put the books back onto the shelves. As I was putting the bundle of papers in my shorts' pocket and buttoning it up, one of the stern librarians walked past.

'No eating near the books!' she hissed, pushing her half-moon glasses back up her nose.

'Sorry,' I mumbled with my mouth full and hurried away. I swallowed the last of the sticky, gluey mess as I reached the door, and gasped in relief. This noise earned me another frown from the librarian, and I decided to escape while I could, before I could be told off any further. I would escape to my home where I could prepare for my meeting tonight.

CHAPTER 10

Several hours later, turning around, I took a last glance at Aunt Hetty's house before I quickly began to walk down Halfway Street. The evening was quite cool, so I was wearing my woolly black jumper for extra warmth. I knew spies wore black too. In my satchel was the bundle of papers, plus a small wrap of money I had discovered under Aunt Hetty's beetle case. The bag also contained all of my clues and notes, my lucky pebble I found in Botswana and the one and only photo I had of my parents and myself. It was taken by a Swedish photographer who had come to visit us in the Amazonian jungle. Mum's face is partly obscured by a tree frond and I have a blue and yellow macaw perching on my head so, all in all, it is not the best photo in the world, but it is a reminder of who I belong to.

I clutched the bag and its precious contents to me as I half walked, half jogged my way to St Tinto's. I knew where the church was as I had played a shepherd in the Christmas carol concert last December. It wasn't a resounding success. One, I didn't want to be a shepherd (I had nothing against them, I just didn't want to 'be' one and didn't really know how to), and two, they not only tried to use a real donkey in the performance, but also real sheep, cows and a grumpy old goat, who began to eat Mary's dress halfway through. It was my first nativity play, and I never wanted to be in one again. As I walked, I passed the occasional late-night dog walker who glanced at me, but I kept on going, despite the occasional 'Hey's!' and 'Are you okay's?' Most of the streets were fairly quiet with everyone safely shut up in their homes. I wished I could be curled up cosily in bed, the distant sounds of Aunt Hetty pottering around lulling me to sleep. But even if I turned around and went back home, no one else would be there; I just had to keep moving forwards.

I reached St Tinto's at seven minutes past ten, and pushed open the squealing churchyard gate. I didn't like being late. It gave me no time to be prepared, but my legs had been more tired than I thought, so I couldn't run much. Big spotlights on the ground illuminated the church building, but they also cast long, ghostly shadows over the bumpy footpath and graves. I looked up at the church, away from the darkness. On every corner and in every crevice were the faces of gargoyles, grinning down at me in the gloom. Twenty-four faces, all grotesque and watching me from above. I stared. One of them moved… not the whole head, just the nose, but it definitely moved and twisted to the right! I took a step backwards, and then another as the nose suddenly whirled off the face and away into the blackness. I'd simply disturbed a quietly resting bat, nothing more terrifying, but my heart was hammering like my chest was wood and each breath a nail as I gripped my satchel strap. I clenched my fists, trying to make myself feel fighting brave, and stepped through the gateway. I began looking for the yew tree but it wasn't hard to spot. It loomed huge on the right-hand side of the church steeple. Stepping off the gravel, I began to weave my way between the tombstones to reach the tree, apologising to the owners every time I accidentally stood on a grave. But now what? I stood under the tree looking around. My hands were still little balls. I thought I could try and use them as weapons if I was attacked, but they looked a bit small. There was nothing but me, a tree, and the bats I could no longer see. Silence, not even the noise of a hooting owl. I shivered, cold despite my extra layer of wool.

'Maisie?' The voice came from behind and I spun around, hating the surprise. In front of me stood the cloaked figure I had last seen taking papers from the chest in Aunt Hetty's study. The face was in shadow as the lights on the church were making bright sparks fly through my eyes.

'Yes.' I felt scared, but tried to sound strong; who was this person? 'What do you want?'

'I'm a friend of Aunt Hetty's...' the speaker paused, '...and Gerald, Margaret, and yourself.'

'My parents? How do you know them? What have they got to do with all this?'

I stood opposite the stranger, waiting for them to reply but I received only silence. I became a bit braver.

'Look. Who are you?' I asked again, 'and why are you involved in all this?'

The figure pulled the hood of their cloak back and stepped forward.

I was blank. There was a person in front of me but I couldn't work out who they were. We didn't say anything. And then as the face smiled at me, I knew.

'Josie!' I gasped. She grinned back at me. I couldn't believe it, it really was Josie! She was one of my parents' assistants who had joined them two years before I left. She was a fellow explorer, born in Scotland, specialising in botany and marine biology. Josie taught me about friends, about spending time with another person doing things with them. I spent my days collecting plants for her to study and helping her to sketch the new discoveries she came across. At night, she would tell me stories of the creatures of the sea, lulling me to sleep as we lay in our small canvas tent. I wasn't expecting Josie here, which was why I didn't recognise her face for a moment until she did the grin I always remembered her by.

'Yes. It's me.' She coughed, clearing her throat, and spitting out a pebble. 'Yuk. The stone is an old trick; it used to be used by blackmailers to disguise their voices. It worked, didn't it!'

She was beginning to sound more normal. 'I couldn't let you know it was me before tonight. It would have put all of us in danger.'

'I didn't recognise you at all. Ever.'

'I thought you wouldn't and that was the point! You've only really seen me when we were in the desert with your parents. Do you remember when I bought a new hat and sunglasses at the market in Whakapapa? You didn't know it was me even though the rest of me was all the same. So I knew I had a good chance that with a bit of disguise, you wouldn't have a clue who was the person underneath. I tried to put on a deep voice and got a huge, hot cloak partly so that Dr Gallows wouldn't recognise me if he had someone watching the house, but it worked for you too. I know it's a silly disguise, but Hetty's friends are so peculiar at times, I figured that I might look more out of place if I tried to look normal. It meant that you wouldn't recognise me and suspect anything was going on with your parents…that you wouldn't worry.' She was talking super speedy fast, and I was struggling to keep up.

'I never guessed it was anyone I knew. But I was worried anyway as Aunt Hetty was behaving so oddly I didn't know what to think. Oh, Josie it's so good to see you.'

I gave her a ginormous hug and she squeezed me the hardest she could. I'd felt so detached since I'd seen Aunt Hetty being taken away, now again I felt like there was someone else there for me and that I could be grounded again.

Josie held me and then stepped away. I saw her face was paler and her eyes had big panda circles underneath. She must be tired like Aunt Hetty was. I wondered how much pressure and stress she must have been under recently.

'We've got a few minutes before we're picked up. I'll tell you as much as I can. It's not good.' She spoke softly.

We sat under the tree and she wrapped her cloak around us. Safe in our soft cave, she began to tell me the whole tale. I wondered how it could be worse than I already thought. But it was.

It wasn't just Aunt Hetty; it all started with my mum and dad. They weren't safe studying bulrushes or hunting alligators, they weren't happy stalking tornados or measuring sea surf. They weren't enjoying the sunshine, or freezing their feet in blistering ice. My mum and dad, Gerald and Margaret, had been taken, kidnapped, stolen, thieved.

'They're here? In England?'

'Yes.'

I felt sort of closer to them knowing they weren't prisoners millions of miles away. But my tummy was still heavy with hurt because they weren't safe. I ached so much it was like my missing them had become a big inside bruise.

They were being held prisoner deep within a network of caves in the south of Cornwall.

'How many caves?'

'I don't know, Maisie, but there's a maze of them.'

Mazes were confusing. If you didn't remember the rights and lefts, you got lost and hit dead ends, and couldn't find your way to the centre or back out again. Being lost in a maze under the earth sounded horrible.

They had been working on a project searching for a big sunken wreck just off the coast. The ship was sailing back from the Caribbean...

'When?'

...in 1654 and had been wrecked during a violent storm, disappearing without a trace, with all of its crew and cargo.

'How many crew?'

'Probably twenty or so. I'm not sure and it's not relevant.'

'But it tells me how big the ship was.'

The ship had been rumoured to have been carrying back several chests of treasure made up of jewels, gold and silver, coins and trinkets, collected from the islands during a two-year trading voyage.

'Trading what?'

'People. Slaves. Also goods.'

'Good what?'

'No, goods. That's things like food and clothes. Furs and cloth. Everyday items.'

'Oh.'

The wreck had been found by three free divers several years ago.

'Why are they free?'

'No, it means they dive without oxygen tanks, they just hold their breath.'

But there was no trace of the cargo. It was generally believed that the ship had been wrecked deliberately on a stormy night, and the treasure taken by smugglers. There was no record of any treasure items turning up anywhere, so it was thought that, somehow, it had been hoarded and forgotten.

'How could you forget treasure?'

'It's not so much forgetting about it, but keeping the hiding place a secret. Then if something happened to the person or people who knew the secret, and they hadn't told anyone else, no one would know where it was.'

'So where is it?'

'That's the point. Your mum and dad were asked to investigate the history of the event, and explore the coast and the surrounding area.'

So they thought that it was hidden somewhere in the cave system just along the coast. My parents had been diving and searching the area around the wreck to try and uncover the mystery.

While they were working, they had been camping in a nearby cove.

'Where was the cove?'

'Near to Kynance, I don't know the name of the inlet specifically. But you can't reach it by road, only by swimming round the cliffs, risking it in a boat, or by climbing down the rocks.'

This meant that they were as close as possible to the ship, well hidden from any prying eyes, and could get on with their explorations undisturbed.

I spoke again. She wasn't telling me the bits I needed to know. She was telling me obvious things, and things that didn't seem important. This question was really, really, really important. 'But they were in England? Here? Why couldn't I see them, why didn't I know?'

'Because, Maisie, their work was so secret. It involved the Secret Service, the British Government. It's not just about what was on board the ship itself, but where it came from too. They were strictly limited as to who they could tell, and that included friends and family. But I do know that they were going to come and stay with you and Hetty once they'd finished. Once the job had been done they wouldn't simply have travelled off again, you would have been able to see them.'

'Oh.' I felt reassured that my parents had actually wanted to see me, that it wasn't their choice I wasn't kept informed. I still felt a bit muddly though. It was horrible to think of them being close and not knowing but then it was sort of comforting too, knowing that they were more nearby than Tonga or Tobago. I had another thought. 'Who is so interested in treasure all of a sudden? And why?'

'It's not just about the treasure in the wreck. There are believed to be some other plans there. Plans and maps. I don't know the full story, so don't ask. But your parents were trusted with the information. Only, now, other people want to get hold of it too.'

I was confused in my tummy, but my head was still following the story so far. Josie continued with her tale.

My mum and dad had been taken by a rival team who were also searching for the treasure.

'Who is the team?'

'We're not sure. But a man called Dr Gallows is in the centre of it.'

'Oh, I know him. He's got fishy eyes and says the same words over and over. Are there lots of other people in the gang?'

'Quite a few. It's hard to know who's really heading it and so we don't know exactly how many people are involved.'

This team, however, were not working for the Government, but for someone else. Someone who knew what the treasure was worth, and also what the plans could reveal. But they needed more information, they didn't have the knowledge to find it on their own. But someone definitely wanted the hoard.

'But why?'

'Because it's worth a lot of money. And possibly to then use the money to finance other operations, that's how these things usually go.'

'He wants an operation? From a doctor? Is Dr Gallows a doctor?'

'No, Maisie. Not medicine. I mean a scheme, or a plot. It's nothing to do with hospitals. I know MI6 are very interested in Dr Gallows specifically, but as far as I know they didn't give your parents any real details, other than to watch out for him in the first place.'

'So they were warned about him?'

'Oh yes. That's why they took precautions to stay as hidden as possible. Not that it made any difference in the end.'

She carried on. When Dr Gallows (or his men) finally found them, my parents refused to pass on the information they had uncovered. Palo had been diving offshore at the time when they were taken so they didn't take him too.

'What did he see when he was diving?'

'I don't know. I wasn't diving with him.'

But she knew he was diving, so why didn't she know what he'd seen? I struggled to work out why people knew some things and not others at times.

Palo got all of the maps and relevant details smuggled out of the camp and posted to Aunt Hetty to keep them safe. The bundle of papers I had received were the most valuable of the documents, containing the entire information imperative to the discovery of the wreck. (This made me feel very important to know they were sitting in my satchel.) Aunt Hetty had originally received the papers, keeping them in the chest. Josie came to take them and put them somewhere safe, but had also sent a few back to me in case she was taken before she could hide them away.

'What?'

Josie just carried on. (Things stopped making any sense at this point but I decided just to keep on listening and figure it all out in my head later on.) Palo had managed to get several of the packages sent off before the gang finally caught up with him and bundled him away too.

In my head I made a list. And it went:

1. Mum and Dad taken.

2. Palo sends important package to Aunt Hetty.

3. Palo sends other packages to Aunt Hetty.

4. Palo gets taken.

5. Josie starts leaving clues in case she and Aunt Hetty disappear.

6. Josie takes rest of papers from Aunt Hetty to put them somewhere safe.

7. Josie sends important package of papers to me.

8. Aunt Hetty gets taken away.

9. I get package.

10. I meet Josie.

The gang had followed the trail the packages had travelled and confronted Aunt Hetty, giving her an ultimatum. If she handed the documents over, Margaret, Gerald and Palo would be released unharmed. If not, she would be taken to be with them, and I would then become their next target.

'Why didn't she hand them over?'

'Maisie! She couldn't risk everything your parents had worked towards. She hoped that somehow, things would work out. This is bigger than your parents, bigger than you and Aunt Hetty. It's about more than all of you. Can you see that?'

'Sort of. But if that was me, you'd say I wasn't thinking things through clearly.'

'That's because none of us have all the facts. But you have to trust Hetty did what she thought was best.'

So, even though it would put her at more risk, Aunt Hetty had made the only choice possible and kept the information hidden, but the gang had kept their word and she had been taken, and she was probably on her way to Dr Gallows' holding place, somewhere near Kynance, this very moment.

A car went quickly past the churchyard, the tyres squealed. Josie spoke in a higher voice. 'Enough. We must move quickly now. There were more cars outside your house earlier today.'

'There are always cars there.'

'Yes, but these were the big black Land Rovers that we've been following for the past few days. I can explain more later but if we don't go soon, they'll come for you.'

'Go where?' I asked. I didn't really want to be taken, but I was a bit more worried about where we were going.

'To Kynance. It's our only chance of ending this. I've got some idea of where they must be being held…and I know how to get rid of Dr Gallows and his men.'

'How?' I was intrigued, interested in the puzzle.

'Can't tell you yet. I need to put a few things in place first. Now, come on!'

She grabbed my arm and we ran together around the back of the church and out through a gap in the hedge.

Josie's cloak streamed out behind her as she ran. Through the hedge there was a road, and waiting there was the big, shiny silver car I'd seen before. I stood, staring. Was this car safe? I didn't want to get in, I didn't know where it would take me.

'Get in,' whispered Josie, urging me forwards. But I couldn't be quick until I had made things feel right. I stopped still and concentrated on counting my steps to the car, trusting in my friend that I would be safe. One, two, three, four and in. I slipped into the big comfy back seat, and before I'd closed the door properly, we were away.

CHAPTER 11

The car sped off down the road and wove its way through the deserted streets in the outskirts of town. Eventually, once I'd counted up to 786, thinking only about the next number and the next, we were out into the countryside and the driver turned around and grinned quickly at me before looking back out at the road.

'Hello!' he said. 'Nice to meet you face to face.'

It was the man with the beard. But as he spoke, I could see him tugging at his face and suddenly the moustache came away in his hands. I nearly squeaked (I don't scream, it's too loud), as I didn't know why half of his face had come off. But he waved it at me and I realised it was false! He didn't have glasses now, and without the beard as well he looked completely different. I definitely wouldn't have recognised him as the same person, but I didn't think anyone else would either. I peered at his reflection in the rear-view mirror. The face felt sort of friendly but I didn't understand why, and then Josie turned around to face me and I saw that she and the man both had eyes that were dark, dark brown, they both had a bit in their cheek that went in as they grinned, and both had two front teeth that overlapped.

'He's your someone related?' I wasn't sure what the word was.

'Yes,' Josie poked him to make him watch the road properly and he turned back round again.

'Milo's my brother and he works as a chauffeur for the rich, famous and good-looking. So I used him to drive me around for a bit.'

'Even though she's not rich, famous or...ow!' Milo stopped as Josie thumped him hard.

'He's been helping me travel about and given me a place to stay for a few nights. But I didn't want anyone to start harassing him too, so I made him use one of his company cars so it couldn't be traced back directly to him. And...'

'And the beard was one I keep in the car for those rich and famous people who don't want to get recognised.' Milo finished off.

'Who?' I asked, my voice finally finding sound.

'Who what?'

'Famous who.'

'Ah, well, that would be telling.' He waggled his finger and I saw the ring again.

'What about the ring though?'

It sparkled tantalisingly. 'This majestic piece of costume jewellery was left behind by a rather glamorous actress with very big hands who I drove to a film premiere several months ago. It looks wonderfully real, but unfortunately has no worth whatsoever. As it fit my ginormous fingers, I just thought it would add more mystery and intrigue to my disguise.'

'It definitely did. So are you coming with us too?' I asked, hoping he was. I liked Milo and I had lots of questions I wanted to ask him about his job. And I thought that more people would definitely be better for chasing Dr Gallows.

'No. I can't. I'm just taking you to the airfield. I have to stay here so that I can send you and Josie anything you need, money and suchlike. And also if your rescue doesn't work…'

'Which it will,' broke in Josie.

'Then I can contact the police. Only as a last resort though.'

'Oh, okay,' I said, not really following but sort of giving up trying. There was too much talk of people doing things in case of other things and then they'd need to do this or that. It was so late, and my mind felt like it wanted to crawl into a duvet and hide. 'So how are we getting to Kynance?'

'My mate's a pilot. He's going to take you up to Aberdeen in Scotland, where you'll pick up some bits that Josie's got to collect. And then you'll fly back down to Bristol,' said Milo.

'Why up then down? Why not just down?'

'You've got to get Josie's packages quickly. And also, if anyone is following you, they'll think you're off in the wrong direction.'

'Why are we going the wrong way?'

'No, it's not really wrong.' Josie spoke, her words clearer than Milo's. 'It's the correct way for us to go. But Dr Gallows' men don't know that.'

'So then we go to Bristol.'

'Yes. It's close-ish to Cornwall, and the airport is big enough that we can land fairly inconspicuously. If we go to a little airfield close to Kynance, we run more risk of being noticed. Dr Gallows is likely to have a network of men who are on the lookout for anything out of the ordinary.' Josie explained. 'From Bristol, we'll drive down the coast and...' I yawned, '...look, it's okay, I'll tell you the rest later. We're nearly at the airfield now.'

The lights from the field and hangar buildings grew closer and I saw four orange windsocks billowing in the night breeze, all blowing to the left side. Milo turned into a small road leading to a grey building made of corrugated iron. He stopped the car outside but kept the engine running.

'Good luck, Josie, and you too, Maisie. I hope you find your parents safe and sound. I'll be here for you.'

I began to ask a question but Josie was opening my door and pulling me out of the car. I didn't even have a chance to thank Milo before we were running towards a small plane that stood close by. I turned and waved at the car as Milo drove off, and heard a thunk thunk thunkthunkthunkwhirrrrrr sound. I turned back around to the plane and saw the propeller turning as Josie pushed me up the steps and clambered in after me.

'Hi Clem. Are the bags on?' Josie spoke to the pilot as she buckled herself in the seat behind him, alongside me.

'Safely in the back. No worries.'

'This is Maisie,' said Josie, pointing to me. I knew I was Maisie, so she must be telling him. The man called Clem didn't turn around and I didn't know what he looked like. His voice was bouncy like a song. Similar to Josie's but a bit different and deeper.

'Hi Maisie. I'll talk more once we're up, but we should get going now, I want to avoid the winds.'

'Okay,' said Josie, 'and Clem, thank you.'

Clem didn't say anything back and started muttering cryptic communications into his headset, talking to someone far away.

The plane sounded like a really noisy purry cat as it rolled along the runway, following the trail of coloured lights. It was a sound I knew well and was comfortable with. It was a sound that made me feel like I was off on an adventure. I didn't like big planes that were like coaches on wings. I liked little planes that were bumpy and noisy and made my nose itch with the tangy smell of diesel. It made me feel like I was back with Mum and Dad. It made me feel smooth inside.

I waited for the lurch and tummy drop of takeoff, but it wasn't until I saw the hangar buildings growing smaller and more distant that I realised we were up in the air.

'Nice flying!' I commented appreciatively. I was used to kamikaze pilots trying to take off in two metres of space, clipping buffalo horns and treetops in the process. English wind was nothing in comparison. If the wind did get worse though, at least my experience of tropical storms had given my stomach the capability to fly in all weathers, and I knew Josie's was the same.

'Maisie?' Josie was talking to me. 'Try to get some sleep. It's really late, and we need to talk through plans, but you should get some rest first.'

I looked at my watch – two-thirty-two in the morning! No wonder I was tired! Josie tossed a stripy red travel rug across to me, and I wrapped it around myself. I watched the lights on the ground grow smaller and smaller, the little dots of colour singing a night-time song, resting me. I fell asleep trying to count stars out of the aeroplane window. I got to 246 before it went dark in my head.

I woke up from a dream where I was trying to eat all of the stars out of the sky before they got too far away, and realised I was starving hungry. The sun shone brightly, and when I looked down from the window I could only see clouds – no clues as to where we were at all. I turned to look at Josie. She was snugly bundled up and fast asleep. The pilot must have heard me moving around.

'Hungry?' he asked.

'Starving! I could eat a horse. Well, I wouldn't want to eat a real horse. It might taste like antelope and I didn't like that. It was sort of hoofy flavour.'

'Well, it's not horse, and it's not very big, but have one of these.' Clem laughed as he tossed me back a cereal bar and I opened it gratefully.

Taking a huge bite, I mumbled my thanks, my mouth full of oats and raisins.

'No problem. We're somewhere over the Welsh mountains – we'll be landing again soon. You slept right through Aberdeen!'

'Bother,' I said. 'I've never been to Aberdeen. Clem, are you Josie's brother as well?'

He laughed again. 'No. What made you ask that?'

'Because your voice does the up and down thing like hers.'

'I'm from Scotland too, but a tiny wee island in the Hebrides.'

'Oh.' I thought for a bit. 'That's sort of the same. But different. I like your voice more. It's got softer edgy bits.'

'Thanks!' Josie had woken up and poked me.

'Finally you're awake. Can you tell me what we're doing next?'

'I will, but not yet.' Josie said, her hand snaking across the gap between our seats to snatch my cereal bar.

'Oy!' I was indignant at her theft, but she just chewed contentedly for a few moments before tossing the last mouthful back.

'I can't say more until we're alone. Not because we don't trust Clem,' she nodded at the pilot, 'but because it could put him in even more danger if he knows any more than he does already. To put your mind at rest though, we're landing at Bristol and then getting picked up by a car.'

That wasn't really enough information to make me comfortable, but at least it was something.

We left Clem and his little plane at Bristol airport, and were eventually picked up by another friend of Milo's, Evan, who drove us down the coast to the very tip of Cornwall. It took three hours and fifty-nine minutes and my legs were wiggly with wanting to walk. Every time we stopped for fuel or sandwiches Josie kept a close watch on anyone who ventured near the car or ourselves. Before long I began to pick up on her habits, so that very soon I was as nervy and jumpy as the jackrabbits I used to track, looking around at everyone and every sound I heard.

We were flying and driving the longest possible detours, to try and avoid any possibility of being followed and the place we were staying at in Cornwall was well away from where we were actually headed. This caused extra stress and confusion for me as I felt like we weren't going anywhere. I could understand why we were doing it – so that as few other people were put in danger as possible and to make it as hard as possible to be followed – but I also just wanted to go the most direct route possible. Anyone who helped us, even inadvertently, could be threatened (or worse) by Dr Gallows and his men.

To keep myself ordered I kept counting numbers, miles, cars and number plates in my head, trying to get some calm amongst the chaos. Josie kept telling me what we were doing and why, which also helped, but I wasn't very happy and my mouth didn't have anything to say for quite a while.

In the afternoon Evan dropped us at the bed and breakfast we were to stay in for the night. Josie had arranged all of the payment before we arrived so we simply had to pick up our key at the front desk before making our way to a tiny room at the very back of the building. Josie and I crashed out on two miniature beds, designed to fit the room rather than the people sleeping on them. Travelling was very tiring and I hadn't had enough sleep the night before. Josie's feet stuck off the end of the bed and she kicked her shoes away, wiggling her toes.

'You're all right, Maisie,' she said, sighing. 'The beds look like they're made for you.' She was right; it fitted me perfectly.

'It's only for one night.'

'Thank goodness!' Josie groaned. 'Although this might be the last actual bed we'll sleep in for a while. It'll be sleeping bags and sand dunes from now on.'

'Sand dunes?' I asked.

'At best,' she replied. 'You'll probably just have to sleep on rocks wrapped up in seaweed.'

'But seaweed's cold. And slimy. And it might have crabs in it. And what if there's a jellyfish?' I was starting to panic. I didn't want to sleep in seaweed.

'No! It's alright, I'm joking.' She sat up and reached over to me.

'Don't joke!' I was cross but when she grinned I felt better and threw a pillow at her. She hurled it back and it was several minutes before calmness regained control again. We had both laughed all of our breath away and I had bits in my side stomach that hurt. It was a happy hurt though.

'Right, Maisie. Sleep time. We'll need it. Tomorrow we begin our proper mission. I've arranged to hire a boat from one of the fishermen so we can check out the layout of the coast. Think you can remember how to steer?'

'No problem, why would I forget?' I said, thinking of all the times my parents had taken me out. We'd sailed around reefs and rocks, small islands and big ones. The last trip I'd made, they'd let me go out on my own, and I went all the way around the Greek island Spetses in a day. They'd kept watch from a pony and trap, tracking me as I went in and out of bays and beaches. I liked little boats; they were like little planes, you could feel the land and air you travelled through. It made the journey real. Where I lived with Aunt Hetty didn't exactly provide many sailing opportunities. There was the lake, and you could hire rowing boats during summer, but rowing on a lake wasn't the same. Especially when the most dangerous thing likely to happen was crashing into another boat and ending up covered in slimy green duckweed rather than falling into shark-infested waters. Sea-sailing again; I couldn't wait. I don't remember much else about that evening, but I'm sure that night I dreamed of the waves and the gentle dipping up and down of the sea.

I woke the next morning to the view of Josie's empty bed, although from the crumpled sheets it looked like she'd attempted to get some sleep there. I was doing the dressing routine, dancing around spiders that were scuttling in between the floorboards, and wondering where we were going to go next, when she re-entered the room.

'You're lively this morning!'

'It's spiders. I don't want to tread on them.'

'All set?' she asked going over to the corner where our bags had been hastily slung the night before.

'Jelly's set. I'm not a jelly.'

'I mean, are you ready.'

'For what?'

'Sailing! Well, motor-boating really. I couldn't get us a sailing boat as it was far too expensive. So I've got us a little motor boat. I chatted to some of the fishermen and it seems that sailing would have been too risky anyway, lots of storms spring up really quickly here and the coast is so rocky, you have to know it like the back of your hand.'

'My hand?' I said, staring at it. I could see pale greeny blue veins, lots of little crisscross wrinkly lines from where my skin bends, and two small freckles.

'No, it means that you have to know the coast really well. And we don't, so a motor boat seems safer.'

I nodded. But I had more things in my head, 'How little is little? And what kind of storms? Why are we going to be any safer in a motor boat?'

'Because it won't capsize as easily, Maisie. Questions, questions, too many questions. Come and see the boat for yourself.' She threw me a rucksack. I opened the top and saw that it contained the contents of my satchel as well as some other bits and pieces I could only catch a glance at, before Josie, hurrying me up, fastened the clasps securely closed. 'Come on.'

We left the room and the spiders to their playground.

CHAPTER  12

I peered over the edge of the jetty. Two small boys were sitting on the side, crab lines and legs dangling over the edge. Every so often, one of them would whip the string up into the air, catching a small wiggle of reddish-brown off the end before expertly flicking it back into the water. The crab went into a bucket, maybe to eat, maybe just to throw back into the sea. I liked crabbing and I wished I had time to join them, but I couldn't stop thinking about my parents. I watched the boys for a few moments before turning my gaze once again to the boat that Josie had hired for us.

'It was cheap,' she said.

'I can see why,' I told her. 'Josie, how are we supposed to travel in this? It doesn't look as if it can float, let alone move.' As if in defiance at my words, the boat lapped gently on an incoming wave, banging into the jetty. It held firm despite the numerous inexpert patches on its hull that threatened otherwise. I could have patched it better. Red paint flaked off with each bump, showing the previous colours of yellow, green and blue that the boat had once been. How old was it?

'It's perfectly seaworthy,' Josie said again (she'd already said it four times). 'Wes has been going out in it every day for fifteen years. He's only letting us have it because he's going away for a few days to visit his daughter in London. We should be thankful, Maisie, look at some of the others!'

I looked. She was right; many other boats in the harbour were in a similar state if not worse. At least ours didn't have any actual holes in the sides. And I'd been in worse boats before. This boat had sides. If I could travel on a raft, watching water pour up through holes and cracks between logs, then I could travel on this.

'Okay.' I said, coming to a settled place in my head. 'Well, shouldn't we get going?'

'Yes, we're just waiting for some...aha! Here comes Wes.'

A brown man was walking unsteadily down the jetty; he looked like he spent all day outside and had gone like the dried leather of goats that I used to see in Kenya. He was almost overbalancing with the weight of a huge oil can held in his right hand. I ran up to help him.

'Off! Off!' He brushed me away like a fly. 'I can manage. I'm not too old yet!' He looked it though, with skin as tough as my dark brown sandals, and hair like white wiry wool. He was a man who'd lived more on the water than on dry land.

Wes poured the fuel into the boat's tank and then stepped back so Josie and I could climb on board.

'See you soon,' he called after us. 'Watch out for storms...and sharks! I want my boat back in one piece!' He winked as he said this so I wasn't scared. It was a sign that Dad had taught me meant someone was teasing. He was also unaware that both Josie and I had come face to face with storms and sharks before (although the shark wasn't man-eating, just fish-eating). I liked sharks, they just swam and ate. Okay, if you got in the way and they wanted a snack, you might be it, but most sharks wouldn't eat you; I was more scared of hippos and crocodiles. They were scary. Anyway, I knew there wasn't much chance of seeing more than a basking shark off the coast here. I didn't like his teasing though.

'Chin up, Maisie,' said Josie.

I raised my head looking up. The sky was blue, and the clouds were floaty fleece soft. It was a lovely day. 'It's nice up there.'

'I didn't mean literally! But yes, it's a beautiful day. Keep cheerful.'

I didn't feel like I had much to be cheerful about considering the whole kidnap situation, but the fact the day was good made me a bit happier.

I grinned at her. 'Sorry.' She smiled back and tugged on the starting motor.

One...two...three pulls and she started! I waved at Wes who was watching Josie weave us in and out of the other boats and off into the open sea beyond. He raised his hand in farewell, and I turned away, looking with Josie towards the horizon.

'What can I do?' I asked.

'You, Maisie, can take the tiller.' I moved over to be next to her and she handed me a small compass as well. 'Keep us heading east along the coast. We've got a few inlets to dodge around, but that's the general direction we need to go in. There shouldn't be much sea traffic, just a few fishing trawlers maybe. Keep an eye out for any stray sailors and kayakers; try not to go too close and then we won't annoy them.'

I watched the needle wiggling and tried to keep it steady on the big, black E. Josie sat back in the boat and closed her eyes. The sun wasn't very far up in the sky, but you could feel some warmth.

'Josie!' I complained. 'You know I want to hear the rest of the story.'

'Okay, okay! Sorry, I didn't know, but also I don't want to be overheard.' She opened her eyes. As she sat up she glanced around as if making doubly certain that there was no one nearby.

'Josie. No one's going to hear you apart from me and the gulls, and maybe some fish that have very good hearing.' I looked up at the sea birds pirouetting above our heads; there were no other boats nearby, and land was slowly becoming more and more distant. 'Well, what are we going to do? How are we going to find them?'

'We don't need to,' Josie said absentmindedly, trailing her hand in the water over the side of the boat.

'Don't need to? They're my PARENTS!'

'No, no. I didn't mean that. I meant I know where they are.'

'You do? Where? How do you know?'

Snatching her hand free from the nibbling mouth of a passing fish, Josie once again stretched out in the boat, and began to talk. I held onto the tiller making small adjustments left or right when we steered off-course.

It seemed Josie had known where they were being kept all along. Well, not precisely, but Palo had worked out where Mum and Dad were being held and had given Josie some directions before he was taken too.

'What directions?'

'I'm telling you.'

The directions began from the cove where my parents had last been based, so all we had to do was reach it and follow Palo's instructions from there. Of course, we didn't know for certain that Palo's guessing was correct, or that they hadn't been moved since, but Josie didn't think it was likely.

'Why don't you think it? I do. I'd move them if someone else had worked out where they were.'

'Yes but Dr Gallows doesn't know that we've worked it out. So he's got no reason to move them. He doesn't know what we know.'

That always seemed to be the case. I thought something, and then forgot other people didn't know my thinking. Remembering that was one too many thoughts to keep in my head.

Josie also said that Dr Gallows and his men would want to keep them near the wreck so they could make the exchange (of people for gold) as quickly as possible.

'But we're not going to give them the treasure, are we?' I asked Josie.

'No. Of course not. That's why we went to Aberdeen, to collect some fake treasure. It's a few pieces of gold-plated jewellery, green glass trinkets, old coins – not real gold or jewels. It's also a mixture of bits and pieces, because I don't know exactly what the real treasure is. They're not worthless, because Dr Gallows would spot anything really bogus, such as if we gave him metal painted gold. But another one of my friends is a curator.'

'You have a lot of friends.'

'I do. I'm lucky.'

'What's curator?'

'A curator. It's a job in a museum or historical house or castle helping to look after it. My friend Calvin makes replica museum artefacts for when the real objects are too valuable to put on display.'

'Isn't that a hoaxer?'

'It's a bit different. But sort of. Yes, he pretends that things are what they're not. Anyway, Dr Gallows won't know the difference.'

'You're sure?'

'Certain. Calvin's one of the best in the world. Experts can't always tell his copies from the real things. And Dr Gallows isn't an expert. He's just a man who wants to make money out of other people's history.' Josie's voice got louder and she hit the side of the boat. I put my hands on my ears and she got quieter. I then checked the boat nervously, still apprehensive about whether it would fall apart.

'So what do we do with the treasure?'

'We have to hide it near the cove within the caves and give Dr Gallows some directions. If we don't hide it, he won't believe it's real. He needs to think he's uncovered the genuine hoard.'

'Where's the real one?' I asked, fascinated.

'I don't know. I don't think your parents do precisely. But they did have maps and directions that could have helped them find it. That's what they sent to Hetty.'

Well. It was all becoming more straightforward the way Josie put it. If everything went as she said, we wouldn't have any problems. However, that also involved Dr Gallows and everyone else doing what we expected. And people didn't always do that, so I wasn't sure whether everything really would go to plan. But if we had a plan, I wanted to know what the next step was, and I asked.

'For now, we keep on sailing down to Kynance. We'll land in a nearby inlet, then hike from there to your parents' camp. From there we'll go into the mine and hide the fake treasure, and try to follow the instructions to Margaret, Gerald, Palo and Hetty.'

'A mine? Like a bomb? A big bomb?' My mind was exploding like a bomb at the thought of it.

'No, like a place where people used to dig things out of the ground.'

'Like the diamond mines in Africa?'

'Yes, that's it. There are lots of old mines here, and some of the tunnels are right on the coast. That's where we'll be going.'

So there was a lot to think about, but not a lot to be done just yet. I only had to keep going east and dodge any sharks or sailors.

Josie and I took turns guiding the boat, the other one resting, eating or watching the horizon for signs of land. Despite its weather-beaten, dilapidated appearance, the boat was actually quite sturdy, and ran smoothly, flipping us through the waves so that spray powdered our faces. I licked my lips. Salt is an itchy taste. When you have a mosquito bite, you want to scratch and when you do it feels so satisfying you want to do it more and more. Salt is like scratching an itch, especially salt on chips. I felt so happy to be out on the sea again, my head was fresh like the breeze on my face. It was so different from the humid mugginess of town life. Things smelled real here, alive. The air smelled like fish splashing and birds flying. Nothing was stifled down, dulled by drains and car exhausts. But I couldn't quite relax. I was only here because my parents and Aunt Hetty were in danger. Real danger. So my head was flying, but the pit of my stomach was all bruised. And something was missing. Even if I wasn't with people, if I knew they were okay, then I was okay. But I knew that they weren't okay and I couldn't be complete. It was as though my worries were was making me less than whole.

I knew I might get lost in my head thinking about the bad things, and that I had a job to do, I had to keep focused, so I concentrated on little things to keep me from thinking about the bad bits; a shoal of silver fish, flipping gracefully through the water below our boat; the boat's spray casting magical rainbows in the air; and the wheeling of crying seagulls dancing high above my head. I had no place I really called home, but these sights and sounds made me feel more reassured than any brick house could.

We boated along the coast for ages and ages. My watch said we'd been out for eight hours and twenty-two minutes and I began to wonder if I'd remember how to walk again when we got to land. It was in the gradually greying evening when Josie announced that we were nearing our destination and I headed the boat inland. Despite wearing caps and sun cream, both Josie and I were sunburned and stiff with the spray of the sea. Both of us were longing to get to the cove so that we could cook some proper food and stretch our legs a little.

'Should reach there in a few minutes,' Josie said.

I looked up again, worried by the clouds that had been gathering for a few hours. The waves out to sea had white bits on them and it was getting rougher. The cliffs got bigger and bigger in front of us. 'Hope so. Don't want to be out here in a storm.'

Josie looked too. 'No. Hopefully the wind will help blow us quickly inland.' As we were speaking, the sun had been covered by the cloud, and the sky began darkening quickly. The wind wasn't gentle any more; it felt fierce, trying to push the sea into shape.

'Come on, come on.' I muttered quietly, willing the boat to go faster as the sea became choppier. Waves began to creep over the sides of the boat, splashing the bags and our legs. Josie hurriedly put the bags under the tarpaulin, trying to protect them from the wet.

'Nearly there!' Josie called to me over the wind. 'Hold on!' There was a loud scrunch as the boat hit the sand, and I toppled forwards, landing in a heap at the bottom of the boat. I'd landed us a bit too fast.

'Come on,' Josie hauled me up and leapt over the side. Knee high in icy water, we pulled, heaved and humped the boat up the beach, tugging it way above the high-tide line to make sure it wouldn't get dragged back out to sea in the middle of the night. Pushing it over onto its side like the back of a turtle, we crawled under the makeshift shelter it made, away from the wind.

'We'll have to stay here tonight,' Josie panted, puffed out from all of the heave-hoing. 'We can't start investigating the cliffs and coves tonight. I don't fancy getting lost in the rocks and sand dunes on the way.'

I imagined us wandering around the rocks, unable to tell the edge of the cliffs from the path. My arms and legs wibbled in a big shiver. But staying here didn't sound too good either. 'What? We need to sleep under the boat? But I thought we were in a tent?'

'We've done it once before.'

'But that was on a tropical island, not on a cold, wet and stormy English beach. You said a tent!' I was starting to panic and my fingers were pulling at the skin on my knees.

'Hey, hey. It's okay, Maisie.' She held my fingers tight and I felt a line of warm running from my hands to my head. 'I know I said a tent, but look outside. It's pouring with rain and icy. We'd go out and get soaked and have no way of getting dry. If we stay here, it's a bit blowy, but at least we're not wet.'

I nodded and she held my fingers for a moment more and then passed me one of the rolled-up sleeping bags. She began to spread out a waterproof groundsheet and we fixed it to the sand as best we could by weighting down each corner with stones. I accidentally picked up a nipping crab with one handful, and squeaked to feel a moving stone. I flung it away only just missing Josie's cheek. The crab turned its back on us angrily and scuttled away to a safer corner. Silly crab. Animals that camouflaged themselves caused me a lot of surprise at times. Especially stupid crocodiles that looked like logs. I'd nearly lost a leg that time though, so a finger nip seemed manageable in comparison.

Finally, groundsheet secured on the floor, we hooked up one long side of it to the upper edge of the boat. We had a shelter, which was nearly rain and wind proof as long as the storm didn't get too big. We could both just about fit in with a bit of room to spare, although getting into the sleeping bags proved a bit tricky. I thought I was fine, and my sleeping bag felt surprisingly big, but when Josie tried to get in I realised each leg was in a different bag and had to untangle myself to sort myself out properly. Eventually we got settled down. I looked at my watch. The hands on the clock had gone round and round; sorting out the boat and our sleeping area had taken two hours and twelve minutes. The sky was really dark now, and we didn't have much option but to try and get to sleep. I hoped the sleeping bags were as waterproof as they claimed, because I could hear a suspicious dripping sound inside our refuge. My tummy gave a humungous rumble.

'I think it's talking!' We laughed. Josie dug around in her rucksack, which she was using as a pillow, and we feasted on nuts, raisins and chocolate while listening to the wind and waves.

'Hope the boat doesn't fall over on top of us.' I muttered sleepily, thinking wearily that the boat was a bit like a tomb.

'Shush, Maisie,' Josie rolled over. So I did.

CHAPTER 13

As so often with coastal night storms, it all blew away. The morning was hazy but bright, light coming through the gaps between the boat and the groundsheet. Much to my surprise I had slept right through, and woke up at five minutes past six, sticky with salt. Josie was still bundled up, her head under her rucksack. I lay for a bit in my bag, liking the feeling of being tightly covered. Duvets and blankets are a bit faffly. They get pulled off and wiggle around when you sleep, and I don't like being uncovered. I have to spend ages wrapping myself up like a mummy usually. Sleeping bags give me edges so I know where I am, which is much easier. My feet soon started fidgeting though, wanting a walk. So I worm-wiggled out of my covers, and went for a wander up the beach to see if there was a freshwater stream running down to meet the sea. I was in luck. In fact, due to the rain the night before, there was a small waterfall tumbling down the cliff into the sandy stream below. I stood below the spray, trying to be brave and ignore the freezing temperature of the water, but every so often a small squeak would escape, and I had to jump up and down to stop my legs from running away from the source of their torture. The cold didn't hurt, it just made my arms and legs prickle and all the hairs on them stand up like a toothbrush. But I knew I'd hate feeling sweaty and grubby even more.

Once I'd finished I felt a lot cleaner although a lot colder and my skin was blue too. I got worried it would go purple, and the purple would make me feel ill. There was still no sign of Josie, so I ran around the rocks trying to warm myself up and change my colour, jumping over stones and playing chase with the seagulls. The seagulls just looked at me and flew away. I couldn't catch them then, I had to pretend to fly on my own on the ground. I wonder why we don't have wings? The sand above the water was littered with the flotsam and jetsam of the sea, old tree branches, seaweed, tarred rope and shells trailing the mark of the tide. There were also some strange items, a blue bucket with a hole in the bottom, one yellow rubber glove, an arm of a plastic doll and a rusty hook. Perhaps the rusty hook had belonged to a pirate? I looked longingly at some wonderful twisty branches of driftwood, and thought how much Dina would have loved them, but there was no way I could carry half a tree trunk back on the boat. I did collect some tiny shells, all pearly like nail varnish, and put them in my pocket for protection, hoping to save them for my keepsake biscuit box back at Aunt Hetty's home.

When I got back to the boat, finally warmed up, Josie was awake and going through her rucksack, sorting out the maps.

'Here,' she tossed them to me. 'See if you can work out where we need to go while I go and wash.' I pointed her in the direction of the waterfall. It was good to feel like I had a purpose and I sat and studied hard.

When she came back, her arms were like mine had been so we gathered up bits of driftwood together and lit a small fire. It was a smoky at first, and when I breathed in all I could taste was old, old trees, but some of the branches from the top of the beach began to burn well. Josie turned pink again and as she began to get out some food for breakfast, I told her about the map.

'I think we're in the wrong cove. I'm not completely sure because this bit of the coast is so wiggly that it's difficult to tell. When I was running around the beach earlier, there was no sign that anyone else had been here for ages. Even if Dr Gallows had taken down Mum and Dad's tent, there would be remnants of a fire, charred wood or stones, or something left. But there's nothing. I think that they must have been in the next cove along. We can get there by boat or by climbing over the rocks. Even at high tide, I think we'd be able to clamber over.'

'Okay.' Josie was nodding. 'It might be better if we leave the boat here and go over on foot. That way, there's even less chance of us being spotted in case any of Dr Gallows' men are on the lookout. It also means we can keep a safe base here.' She tore open a foil package and tipped the contents into a collapsible saucepan she'd had stashed somewhere. Adding some water from a bottle, the contents began to rehydrate themselves into something which looked like slush. One of the things I hadn't missed about being with my parents was the dehydrated packet food they kept for emergencies. Most of the time we had been able to eat local food, whether we'd bought it at a market or picked it ourselves. But there would always be days when that wasn't available or wasn't enough, and then out the silver packets would come. Dad told me that explorers used the food all over the world, and up in space they had freeze-dried food. Space was somewhere I hadn't been. I used to pretend to be an astronaut sometimes. I would imagine being hundreds of miles above the earth, floating amongst the stars, finding new planets. If I did that, somehow, the packet food would taste a little bit more bearable. I tried to do it now, but Josie kept talking and distracting me.

'Maisie? *Maisie?* Are you listening? I asked you to pass the spoons.'

'I was in space. Where are they?' She was pointing but I couldn't see. There were bags and rocks and nothing that was silver like a spoon.

'There. Come on, I'm hungry!'

'Where?' I couldn't see them. I wanted to do what she said, but I couldn't and that made me feel sick.

'They're red and plastic.'

'Oh.' I reached out and grabbed them from beside the rucksack. 'I was looking for a metal spoon.' When she described what they looked like, I could see them. Josie stirred the spoons in something grey and mushy.

'Don't wrinkle your nose like that. You look like a disgruntled rabbit. Try it. It's fruit and oats. A sort of appley porridge. You need to eat it anyway because I don't know when we'll next be able to get hot food. Enjoy it while you can.' She dug in with her spoon and handed one to me.

I took a tentative mouthful. 'Whoo! Hot.' I exclaimed, trying not to spit it out.

'Well, blow on it to cool it down then. Honestly, Maisie, what are you like?'

I was more careful with my next bite. I had to admit, it was actually quite tasty. Not really porridge, but there were definite apple bits. It didn't matter that I couldn't imagine myself into space because the food was bearable enough here on earth. We ate until the pan was empty, and then cleaned it in the stream, and carefully put the fire out. Then the groundsheet was taken down and packed up with sleeping bags. And after all that, we were ready to be on our way.

'Won't the boat be spotted?' I asked Josie.

She frowned. 'Maybe, it's a bit bright, but I don't know what else we can do.'

I looked around and I saw that the beach was covered with lots and lots of seaweed. Some book stories came back to me. Books are very useful sometimes. 'Look, I once read about some people who had to camouflage their boat, so they covered it with seaweed to look like a rock. I think they buried themselves in sand too, and covered up with the seaweed. And it worked; the enemy didn't notice them or the boat at all. One of them even got trodden on!'

'Well, I don't think we need to hide ourselves, but it's a good idea for the boat. Well done, Maisie!'

We both spent fifteen minutes dragging long armfuls of weed over to the boat and draping it over the hull. I tried hard, but it was difficult not to shudder at the slimy, slippery feel. I had to keep telling myself 'It's for Mum and Dad,' over and over again to try and distract myself. Soon, the red paint was barely visible.

'There, I think we're done. And if we can't see it when we come back, then just remember that it's straight in line with that tall pointy rock sticking out of the cliff.'

We began to make our way over the rocks towards the cove next door. Luckily the tide was still quite low, and apart from when I slipped into a shallow rock pool at one point, we managed to keep our feet fairly dry. The climbing was hard because the rocks were damp, but thousands of barnacles sticking fast to the surfaces made it easier for our feet to grip on. Each barnacle looked like a mini volcano and I tried to see if I could make the barnacle creature come out. But even if I prodded it really hard it wouldn't. Barnacles must be shy. My rucksack threatened to overbalance me backwards at one point and I had to cling on to some limpets to upright myself. (I think the proper words are 'right myself' but I wasn't wrong I just wasn't upright.) I silently thanked the limpets and apologised if I'd hurt them at all; they wouldn't hear me, but at least I knew I'd said it.

It wasn't an easy time. The walking was hard, and the fear of what could lie ahead and the safety of my parents stayed in my head, lurking like the evil crocodiles I detested. I tried to distract myself by counting as many different types of shells and sea and rock creatures as I could see. I got all the way up to fifteen, including a red squirly anemone that looked just like a wine gum, and a tiny teeny shrimp that darted across the water when my shadow moved past, and then I looked up. We'd rounded the corner, and could see the stretch of cove ahead. And there, in one corner, was a brown and green tent looking just as I'd expected it to. We'd found the right cove! I looked over to Josie and we grinned at each other. The tent was a sign that we were on the correct trail, heading in the right direction. I felt a firework inside, like a fizzy sparkler. We both started bounding over the rocks; I so, so wanted to get there and Josie did too. Her legs were longer and she got ahead of me. Sometimes I wished I could turn into a cheetah, or have long, lollopy legs like a giraffe to cover distances quicker. Halfway to the tent, suddenly Josie stopped and crouched down. I carried on.

'Get down!' she hissed quietly, and so I immediately stopped, banging into a rock, and knelt too. I rubbed my ankle. Bother Josie. She could have told me to stop in a better place where I wouldn't have knocked myself.

We were amongst the big rock boulders, and I stayed behind one until she worked her way closer to me, dodging in and out of the shadows.

'Why are we hiding?' I whispered to her.

'Well, we don't know if there's anyone keeping watch. I got carried away when I saw the tent. We need to be more cautious. I want us to stay here for a few minutes, just in case we can see anything suspicious. If everything looks okay, then we'll carry on, but if it doesn't...'

'Yes?'

She hesitated. 'We'll just have to decide that when we come to it. Now, let's stay quiet and watch.'

We only waited there for three minutes, but it felt like three hours had passed when we finally moved forward again. I could see the fabric of the tent fluttering in the breeze. It looked so deserted, so abandoned and there was no other sign of life anywhere. When I looked at Josie I could see her eyes darting left and right, spying out any possible hiding places where people could be lurking, but there was nothing. There was no one but us on the beach. When she stood up I presumed it was okay for me to do so as well. My legs had cramped in position, and Josie had to haul me upright. I leaned into her, and she gave me a firm hug. She never seemed to forget I hated prickly touching.

'It's going to be okay, Maisie. I wish I hadn't had to bring you, but I couldn't leave you alone in Hetty's house not knowing what was going on.'

'I wouldn't have let you. Even if you'd never met with me behind the church, I would have tried to work things out on my own. I don't want to be here, but I want everyone to be safe. I want everything to be right again. But why us, Josie? Why do we have to be the ones to find them? If they were doing Government work then shouldn't they be finding them?'

We carried on walking as Josie answered. 'It's not that simple. I wish it was. And I wish I had all the answers but I don't. All I know is that the work your parents were doing…lots of people were interested in it. Lots of people, from lots of countries. Working for the Government doesn't necessarily mean that the Government will work for you.'

'What does that mean?'

'For example, if things went well, they would acknowledge what they'd asked your mum and dad to do, and get the rewards and recognition. But if they don't go well…then they pretend they were never involved in the first place. Your parents were willing to go along with that because they never expected things to go so drastically wrong. They thought that they had enough backup and support to protect them. Only…well, here we are. On the rescue trail. It's you and me, Maisie.'

'And Milo,' I reminded her.

'Yes, Milo if we need him. We're lucky, really. If anything happens to us, at least Milo will know the whole story. And, ultimately, we can go to the police. But that has risks of its own.'

'I thought police were safe? They're supposed to help people.'

'Yes and nearly all police people are safe. But not always. Just because you do a certain job doesn't mean you're a nice and honest person.'

We carried on in silence. I was heavied by the thought that we could be 'disappeared' too, and I wondered why people would pretend to help others, but not really. Josie's words weren't cheerful ones, but my head couldn't come up with any other ideas. We were doing what we had to do.

Nearing the tent, I ran on ahead, suddenly desperate to get to something that belonged to my parents. It was so long since I'd seen them, but coming to a place where they'd recently been helped me to feel closer to them again. Everything on the tent was zipped and fastened. The breeze circling inwards from the sea caught the ashes from a long-dead fire, dusting them around my feet. I knelt before the entrance, wanting to go inside, but feeling as though I was going into a space that wasn't mine. I didn't know what to do, or how to let myself enter. I heard footsteps behind me as Josie caught up. I looked up at her and she nodded gently.

'Open the tent.'

It gave me an instruction I could follow, something I knew how to do. I slowly unzipped the tent door. Thinking about it now, the most sensible thing would probably have been to rush straight in, hastily search for any possible clues, and get out of there and into more sheltered surroundings as quickly as possible. Although we hadn't seen anyone, the tent was very exposed, and we would have been easy to see. But I couldn't rush in. The tent seemed like it was the last real life link my parents had made, and I wanted to stay with it, feel a connection with them for as long as possible. When I was apart from them, I couldn't imagine them. I didn't think about them and have moving pictures in my head of what they might be doing. It was the special things I kept in my biscuit box at Aunt Hetty's that helped me to conjure up pictures of where we'd been, things we'd experienced. Some of the precious things I kept included my volcano rock from Mount Vesuvius. Touching and holding that reminded me of the hut we'd stayed in together during the rains. Smelling my cinnamon bark from Sri Lanka reminded me of Mum showing me how they stripped it from the cinnamon tree to sell at the markets. This tent was theirs; being near it meant I could think back to all of the other places where I had seen them using it. Rushing in would only have destroyed the bond, the link to them. I don't know if Josie understood but she didn't hurry me along. I knew she loved my parents too.

We took our time and climbed into the tent, zipping the door shut behind us. Although coming out again would be risky, we could at least stay hidden while we searched the inside. The interior was typically neat and orderly. Everything had its place; everything was safely stored away so that it could be found whenever it was needed. It was one of Dad's golden rules – return everything where you found it. I learned quickly that it made a lot of sense that if you took something from somewhere that was where it should go back to. I was rarely told off when I was younger, but there was one time when my dad became so mad at my actions that I had to clean his hiking boots spotlessly clean from swamp mud every night for thirty-one days. The reason for this tortuous task was that I had wanted to see if I could count glow worms one evening, so I borrowed his binoculars from his rucksack to get a closer look. After staying up half the night and reaching a grand total of 897, I was so tired that I fell asleep with them around my neck, and only awoke once he had already left the camp the next morning. I thought nothing of it as his rucksack wasn't there, so I couldn't return them to him. I just put the binoculars safely in my tent to put in his rucksack when he got back. But he didn't. Hours passed and it got darker and darker, and eventually one of the monkey men (he studied monkeys, he wasn't an actual monkey) went out to look for him. They returned at about ten o'clock, a dangerous time, after twilight when the big creatures began to come out. Dad had lost his way tracking the trails of a lemur colony and climbed a tree to see which direction he should go in. He went to get his binoculars to get a closer look…and they weren't there. He had to guess his way, and keep climbing trees to check that he was on the right path. It took him hours longer than it should have. When he explained to me how lost he could have got, and that he might have been attacked by a jaguar or got lost in the forest and never found, I began to realise that he could have been in serious trouble. I always remember this now if I want to borrow something and I try to make sure I always ask first. I don't want anyone to be got by jaguars because of me.

There seemed to be two of everything in the tent. Two sleeping bags, two torches, two thermos flasks, and two copies of *The Mining Maps of Cornwall* (both very dog-eared and smudged with dirt and grime). It was the fact that there were so many pairs of everything that made one thing stand out. Tucked into the left-hand tent pocket, next to an open packet of man-sized super strength tissues and a half-eaten bar of Kendal mint cake, was a rock. It was dark with a light grey band running through it, and comfortably fitted into the palm of my hand. Rocks with bands all the way round them are supposed to be lucky. I'm not sure what it is about the band that makes it lucky, but it is nice to look at. Your eyes can go all the way round the rock and end up where they started. Both of my parents were forever picking up odd and peculiar trinkets and objects, either for souvenirs or to study later on. Getting distracted, I made myself stop looking at it, and was about to put it back when Josie stopped me.

'Wait, Maisie.' She took hold of it and slipped out an intricate pocket knife. There were so many assorted gadgets on it, it took her a few moments to open up a screwdriver, bottle opener, miniature saw and a long pointy proddy thing that I wasn't sure of, before she arrived at a magnifying glass. She squinted through it for a moment before exclaiming, 'I knew it!'

'Knew what?' I tried to peer over her shoulder. The band running through the rock suddenly glinted off the reflection of the glass. 'Is it silver? Are we rich?'

'No you daft thing. It's tin. And even if it was silver, it would probably be worth about five pence.' She folded the glass so it was hidden again and sat back. 'The directions Palo sent me indicated that they were being held in a network of tunnels that were connected to the nearby tin mine. I don't know if your parents left this here deliberately. They knew that they were at risk and may have tried to leave a clue that wouldn't be easily picked up by the wrong people. Or it could be a simple coincidence. But it seems too much of a coincidence to just be chance. It gives me more confidence that Palo has set us on the right path.'

'I think it's a clue. Clues help us, and this has been helpful. So we carry on following them?'

'We do. But let me show you where. I'll get the map that Palo has drawn.' She got out something from her rucksack. It was a piece of paper, folded four times and all raggedy on the edges as if a mouse had been having it for lunch. On the paper were lots and lots of lines, a few circles, and some dots too. It reminded me of some of Dina's paintings only a lot more grey and boring, but it didn't look like a normal Ordnance Survey map at all. She then got out one of the *Mining Maps of Cornwall* and started comparing them.

I like Ordnance Survey maps but they are hard to understand. Ordnance Survey maps are the big huge foldy ones that show you hills and roads and horse paths and post offices and army camps. You open them up and they cover the floor and then you turn them over and there's even more map on the back. But then you try to put them away and fold them up again and you can't and you get told off for not putting the map away properly even though it was the map that wouldn't fold rather than you that wouldn't fold it.

There are also lots of lines and numbers on them telling you the height of hills and where the edges of places are. And those make it more confusing. If I look at one whole side of the map, I can't see anything, all of the colours and lines and letters just blur. But if I start by focusing on one small thing like a particular road or footpath, I can plot a journey. My mum made sure I could do that, because if you are able to read maps you can find your way in and out of places and I don't like being lost. So much information makes my head hurt, and trying to train my eyes to follow one specific route is like asking my nose to only smell one food in a restaurant. Reading maps takes all of my concentration and I usually end up cross-eyed and frazzled.

My parents usually had to chart their own maps rather than following one someone else had made, as so often the places they seemed to go had never been mapped or even travelled before. They taught Palo how to chart maps too, and even though his map had been hastily scribbled on a piece of notepaper the lines were clear and I could start to see that what he'd drawn matched a small section on the other map Josie had unfolded. Josie talked it through with me, her finger moving between maps as she spoke. I had to keep half listening and half looking as I couldn't follow both things at once. She ended up repeating herself twice until I got it.

'There's a break in the cliff face just around the corner from the tent. If we go in there, we should find a grille at the end of the cave, this will lead to a passageway winding through the cliff itself, and then down into the earth, joining up with the network of tunnels from the tin mine.' Josie traced the way. 'Palo thought your parents were being held in one of the old mining cages that they used to use to lift up the miners back to the surface.'

'Like a bird cage?'

'Yes, but bigger, like a cage for an animal at a zoo.'

'I don't like zoos, animals shouldn't be shut up even if they do bite.'

'I know, but it's not actually a cage from a zoo. It's just a lift, like the ones in tall buildings, but a metal cage rather than a solid box.'

I screwed up my face. I didn't like lifts either. They went up and down and you couldn't see the up or the down. It just happened.

'These lifts are disused now but kept in a recess near the main mine chamber itself. There must be a way up to the surface from there.'

'So Palo and Aunt Hetty must be there now too.' I contributed.

'Well, yes, logically. But we don't know that Dr Gallows works logically. Who knows what goes on in that crazy brain of his?'

'Crazy brain!' I liked the sound of these words. 'But he's got no reason to suspect anyone has tracked him this far has he? I mean, he knows about you and me, but he doesn't know that Palo got a map out to you. So he must think he's safe.

'Yes.' Josie sounded definite.

Before we left the tent we divided the torches, extra food and copies of the mining map between us. The torches were spare in case ours broke and the extra food was stored away for emergencies (although I hoped there wouldn't be any). And, as Josie said, the maps were better than any we currently had, and it wouldn't do to get lost down there. I went spiralling into thoughts of getting lost in miles and miles of mazes of tunnels, never finding the light, never finding the way out! You'd be under the houses and people and normal life but couldn't get back to it. I wasn't sure how I would feel about being underground, it wasn't somewhere I'd been much before. It was going to be strange not seeing the sky or feeling the wind. A tug on my arm from Josie brought me back into reality. We were packed up. We were ready to travel down. I had to be brave.

The first challenge appeared to be to get out of the tent safely without being seen. It could have posed all sorts of problems, but we were in luck again. Josie cautiously stuck her head out of a small gap in the zip, looked all around, and then edged her way out. She disappeared and I could just hear her feet stumbling over rocks and fading into the distance. I looked at my watch. I was to give her exactly two minutes, and then follow. That would be enough time for her to get to the shelter of the cliff face and be able to properly look around to check there was no one else there. After exactly two minutes I was to follow unless I heard a loud cawing seagull cry. On her months at sea spent whale watching, Josie had worked on perfecting her sea bird calls. It wasn't really the situation she expected to be using it in, but her impression of a gull would do very well as a warning signal. I had wondered how I would tell the difference between her and the real gulls, and asked her what specific gull she was going to be, but she assured me that she wasn't *that* good and couldn't yet do different gull species.

The second hand on my watch slowly circled round (it counts the seconds but it's actually the third hand and it's not even a hand, it's just a moving stick). Once, twice, two minutes. I paused, there was no loud gull call, no cry of 'Stay away!' I took a deep breath, looked for one last time around my parents' home, and ran. The distance between the tent and the cliffs was short and as my feet slipped and slid on the rocks it felt like forever. But at last I was there, in Josie's welcome hug, then being hurriedly hustled round the corner and into the cave.

'Well done. First difficulty over. And you didn't even have to suffer my terrible seagull call.'

I was doing the in in in in breathing thing again, from running hard and from being scared, but I gradually began to slow it down, becoming calmer. My eyes were trying to adjust to the light, or lack of it. I could only see bright and dark, I couldn't tell what things really looked like at first. When you look at the sun and then look away, things look black even though they're not. That's what it was like going into the cave from the outside. Over a few seconds though, it all started to be seen, and Josie also put her torch on which helped. The cave was dingy, dark grey walls casting long shadows on the sand, turning it to the colour of mud. And it smelled! The colour smelled damp, and it really smelled of rotting seaweed, of long-dead fish and bird carcasses. I wrinkled my nose. Josie laughed.

'Oh Maisie! It does stink though, doesn't it! If it gets too bad we'll tie our scarves round our noses and mouths, but just try to breathe shallowly and get used to it.'

How did you breathe shallowly? I figured you had to open your mouth a little and take tiny sips of air. But that made me feel like my chest was popping out. So I just held my hand over my nose and breathed normally in the end. Although my nose was still twitchy, the more time I spent in there the more I got used to it. But I didn't want to get used to it. It felt like the cave smelled of death and dirt, of the endings of life, of hope that had long died. I wanted to get out of there as quickly as possible, before my hope departed too.

We began to search for the grille which would indicate the opening to the tunnels. I thought it would be like a grill pan only without the pan bit, all metal lines crossed with each other. Shining our torches around, it was difficult to spot the metal grid. The light beam kept reflecting off the water on the wall, the glinting light gleaming like metal. Every possible crevasse held nothing. Josie had no more luck than me. The cave still felt stifling, and I couldn't stop smelling the smell which was making me feel like I was all rotting away inside. I was desperate to get out, but I couldn't just walk outside, I would have been walking away from all of the people I loved, and even though this was all so horrible, I had to make myself put up with it. I knew we had to keep going.

I moved nearer Josie and we began to strip slimy mouldering seaweed from the walls. It was awful, the slithering tendrils seemed to wrap themselves around my fingers, pulling me closer, trying to ensnare me in their grimy grip. I carried on, determined to beat the weed, when I noticed Josie's movements quicken.

'What?' I looked over at her.

'I think I've found it!' her voice rose in excitement, and we worked together, heaving handfuls onto the floor. A few minutes later it was clear she was right.

'Josie, you're magic!'

'Not quite, but definitely lucky. I thought we were going to have to give up there.'

'Me too. But not now, it's really there. We must be on the right path.'

Our excitement gave us both a new burst of energy, and we had cleared the grid free of weed in minutes. It looked like I thought, only a lot bigger, which made sense as we had to go through it to enter the mines. You wouldn't fit in a normal-sized grill pan. It was screwed into place, but years of seawater had rusted the screws free, and pulling together, we heaved the grille away from the wall and onto the floor of the cave. A deep, dark mouth gaped at me.

I sat back on my heels. 'And we need to go in there?' I knew the answer. But the dark seemed so ominous, so forbidding. I didn't want to go anywhere near it.

Josie understood, and she touched my shoulder gently. I wriggled away quickly, the touch making me shudder. It wasn't comforting at all. Josie grasped my arm harder and it felt better. 'You know we have to, Maisie. And with torches, the dark won't seem so bad. And remember, we've got each other.'

A sudden thought occurred to me. 'But Josie, why was the grid screwed shut? Why wasn't it loosened, if people have been down here before us?'

'I can only suppose that your parents didn't get the chance to try out this entrance, and that Dr Gallows is using one of the other ways in. There are so many different openings and exits, and such a maze of tunnels, there's no way of knowing which one they're using. It's lucky we've got a map, I wouldn't fancy trying my chances in this labyrinth without one.'

'Labyrinth?'

'It's another word for a maze. There's an ancient Greek myth about a minotaur in a labyrinth.'

'A minotaur? We're in a mine, is it something that lives in mines?'

'No, it's a monster, make believe. It's not real. I'll explain another time, Maisie.'

'Do you know where we're going to hide the treasure?' I tried to get back on track.

'There's a small recess in one of the tunnels…hold on,' she got the mining map out of her rucksack and spread it out on her knees. Studying it for a few seconds, she pointed. 'Here. See? It was a section they dug into one of the walls so that the miners could take cover when one of the mine trucks was pulled past, so they wouldn't get run over. We're here at the moment…and the recess is just a short way down towards the left. Then we'll need to backtrack and head right, up the tunnel system, and hopefully towards your parents.'

I could follow Josie's finger, but the map itself was just a web of passageways, layer upon layer of tunnels. This was even more confusing than an Ordnance Survey map, a copy of what looked like one of the original layouts of the mine. How did you know which one led to another? I stared hard, but it didn't get any clearer.

Josie saw I was uncertain about what she was showing me. 'Look,' she said, handing it over. 'You have this one; I've got the other copy in my bag. You should have this on you anyway, just in case we get separated, without it, you'd be stuck.' She spent a couple of minutes talking me through the basics, until I felt a bit more comfortable about how to work out which tunnel was which and what was a dead end. All the while, the black gaping hole of the tunnel stared at me, taunting me. It was as if it was saying, 'They're just down here! Come and see!' But it also looked like it would swallow me up. I wasn't sure if it was a good or a bad thing. Before I could see, I knew we had to make sure we both had the best possible chance of getting out of there once we'd gone in and I tried to concentrate hard.

Finally, the map reading sorted, we were ready to go. We both had our torches fixed to our heads to enable us to have our hands free to hold maps and cling onto the rock walls if the surface became slippery. I was hoping that it would make me feel a bit more like an experienced caver, but it didn't seem to be working, I just felt like Maisie with a head torch. Josie went to crawl into the hole.

'Wait!' I said quickly. She turned back. 'Just...I just want to say, good luck.' I wanted to say more but I didn't know what words would say my thoughts. I think Josie knew that, and came and gave me a hug.

'It's okay, Maisie. Just keep close, follow me and stay quiet. Let me know as soon as you have a problem with anything or notice anything wrong. We're in this together.'

I pulled away and gave a grin that was a bit wobbly. 'Go on then! I'll be right behind you!'

Crawling headfirst into the unknown darkness was one of the most terrifying things I've ever had to do. I watched as Josie's head, upper body and then legs disappeared in front of me. I knew I should follow. But I just stood there; my feet wouldn't move. With my head I was willing them, saying 'Come on feet, move!', but they wouldn't obey. It was as though I'd become part of the rock, moulded to the floor like a human stalagmite.

'Move!' I desperately willed my feet, but they still refused to budge. Then I remembered something Dad had once told me.

'Sometimes you need to pretend. When you're in a position and you feel stuck or when you don't know where you are and what to do, become someone else. Be someone who will know and who will be able take you out of it. And when you're out of it, become yourself again.'

Right, I thought. Who would know? And suddenly, I was no longer Maisie. I was an SAS soldier, about to start a caving expedition. Going down into the depths, under the surface of the world. On a mission to save.

I shucked my rucksack back into a more comfortable position, squared my shoulders, and counted down.

'Agent Maisie? Three, two, one and off!'

CHAPTER 14

The walls of the tunnel were tight, squeezing against my shoulders, my legs. Using my elbows and tips of my boots I shuffled and pulled myself forwards. Rocks and pebbles and grit were under my hands and grating my knees. If my head brushed the roof of the tunnel, it all came down in my face as well. I spat sandy muck, keeping my mouth shut as much as possible. My light showed the bottom of Josie's feet up ahead, and the damp, grey walls, the same as the cave. I couldn't look up, there was no room to turn. Panic began in my stomach, turning it into a churning, heaving wormy mass of nerves. And then I remembered, I wasn't Maisie, I was a soldier. And I pushed the fear away, focusing on moving forwards centimetre by centimetre. Thinking only about exactly what every part of my body was doing to get myself through. Right arm, right leg, left arm, left leg, right arm, right leg and so on and so on and so on. I knew that the tunnel would open up very shortly (as long as the mine plans were correct) and, sure enough, suddenly Josie's feet disappeared from view. At the same time, she spoke softly, 'Maisie? In a second, you'll come to a slight dip, feel your way forwards, and let yourself slide down carefully.'

I came to the dip as she spoke, and felt the surface of tunnel slope down forwards. Trying not to tumble headfirst, I eased my way down, and then felt Josie's strong arms guiding me. All of a sudden, I was standing up, the space around a wonderful relief from the tight cocoon I'd been trapped in. We were in the first cavern. It was about two metres wide and high, and looking up, I could see long stalactites hanging down from the roof. Nearby were half-carved names and markings, graffiti from the old miners who used to work down here, day in, day out. I looked and wondered what Bill and Sam and John had once done, but then Josie took my arm.

'This way. Watch your feet, I don't know how slippery the floor will be. We need to be quick, but we don't want to fall. Take it steady, keep your wits about you.'

'Wits? Isn't that being funny?'

'No, it means be aware of what's going on. And keep moving. I don't want us to be down here any longer than we need.'

There were two tunnels leading out of the cavern, and we moved towards the left-hand one. It was down here that we were going to put the treasure. The tunnel was narrow, but tall enough to walk through – at least it was for me, Josie had to crouch a couple of times to duck under low overhangs. Water continuously trickled down the walls and pooled on the floor. Although I tried to be focused, I couldn't help thinking about all the other feet that had passed through this way, the journeys they had taken. And how different our journey was today. There was no sound apart from our footfalls and the dripping of water. No outside noise reached in. It felt like we were cut off from the world.

We walked for ten minutes, following the same route and not taking any detours off into the small side passages that came up occasionally, when we reached the ladder. The tunnel continued forwards, but Josie stopped.

'This is it. Just up the ladder is the recess, we need to leave the treasure there.'

She looked again.

'Well, okay, not really a ladder.'

She was right. The rust had eaten away at the slats; continuous water dripping down over the decades had created great holes in the metal. But the spikes driven into the walls either side, holding the sides of the ladder in place, were solid.

'Josie, we can climb up those, they'll give some sort of foothold.'

'I'll climb up. Not you. It's too risky.'

She was firm, but it made no sense. 'Look. I know you don't want me to get hurt but it's silly. I'm lighter. If anything's going to hold, it will do so under my weight rather than yours. Plus, you can give me a boost up which will take me halfway there.'

She looked uncertain, but couldn't really argue with my reasoning. I was here with her, already in danger, it made no sense to try and start getting overprotective now.

'Right. Put on my rucksack first, and hand me yours. It's heavy, but it'll be lighter coming back down. The package you need to leave is in the bag and well wrapped. Just leave it as it is, obviously displayed. The people who are going to be down here looking for it need to see it.'

'What about the water, will the dampness spoil it?'

'It won't be there for long enough. Or it shouldn't be. Don't worry about that.'

While I sorted out changing my pack, she made sure the spikes lower down the wall at least were secure, and she steadied herself. I stepped into her outstretched hand and she lifted me up.

Her voice squeaked slightly with the strain of my weight, 'I'll hold you until you're sure that the fixings higher up the wall are safe.'

I grabbed hold of the metal and tried to move it. It wouldn't budge. I couldn't be certain that it was absolutely fine, but there was nothing else to do. I called down to Josie, 'Okay, I'm moving up.'

The tips of my boots scrabbled and then firmly took hold on a support. My fingers similarly scraped at the wall before finding a ledge. I wasn't flat against the wall, but I wasn't far off. The light on my head was little use, but because Josie was underneath me, looking up, her light glowed on my surroundings. Back in my SAS soldier mentality, I took each hand and each foot at a time. My right arm would reach up, find the next handhold, make certain it wasn't too unsafe, and take hold. Then my left foot would follow, finding the next ledge to rest on. And then my left arm would move, and then my right foot. Gradually, little by little, I began to move upwards. My fingers were aching with the cold, the metal underneath them chilling them to the bone. But a soldier wouldn't think of that; he would think only of his mission ahead. Get up the wall and leave the treasure, then down the wall and on towards the rescue. Hand by hand, foot by foot, I got higher. It felt like I'd been climbing for hours, but it could only have been a few minutes (I wanted to know how long but couldn't look at my watch properly; wanting to know the time when I couldn't was like an irritating itch) when my left hand, floundering above my head, felt not metal, but a stone ledge. The knowledge that I was nearly there gave me a new burst of energy, and using a great huff of strength, I heaved myself up and onto the ledge. I was breathing hard, but managed to pant out to Josie, 'I'm here. Give me a second and I'll start back down.'

'Well done!' She clapped a little and I knew she was pleased. 'Take a few minutes if you need it. Make sure you feel alright to come back down. It'll be tricky and I don't want you to slip and fall now that you've come so far.'

She was right. I needed a moment to collect my breath and my thoughts. The climb up had been short but hard and going back down was in many ways more risky. I sat on the ledge and took off my rucksack. There was space for several Maisies up here, but there was only me, and Josie felt a long, long way away. I imagined the mining men up here, eating their lunch, those thick Cornish pasties, half filled with vegetables, half filled with jam, a main course and pudding in one. It would taste very odd if you had a mouthful of both at the same time. Although peanuts and jam work together, they're a sort of tickly tongue and then a nice scratch after. And I also like cheese and jam. But I don't know why, it just matches. I wasn't sure either of those fillings would work in a pasty, but it didn't matter, I didn't like pasties. I liked pastry, and I liked the middle, but I didn't like hidden food. Pies and pasties didn't let you know what they were just by looking, and you couldn't be sure what you would taste. I didn't expect the miners cared about that, but it did seem very important to me. How could they ever have imagined that a Maisie with a pack full of fake treasure and maps would one day be sitting there thinking about them, though?

I'd been sitting long enough and my bottom had gone. Cold makes bits of you disappear sometimes.

'Back to work, Maisie.'

I looked around, and then realised the words had come from my own mouth. My SAS soldier personality must have kicked in without me realising it. But it was true. I needed to think about now. About the treasure.

My frozen fingers had difficulty in unfastening the clasps on the rucksack. But with perseverance the clips loosened, and groping around in the inner contents my fingers fastened on the package at the bottom. It was bulky and heavy and I needed two hands to lift it out. The contents were wrapped in some sort of hessian or burlap sack. The material was stained and tattered, marked by dirt and dust and it looked like the edges were greasy with age. I knew it wasn't old, but it certainly looked it. I realised that there was no point in leading Dr Gallows to the hoard and expecting him to believe in it if it was left wrapped neatly in modern-day paper and sticky tape. The packaging had to be as authentically aged as the contents. Placing it on the ledge, I resisted the temptation to peek inside. I wanted to see what Dr Gallows was getting so excited about. But I knew I couldn't. And anyway, it wasn't the real treasure. One day maybe I would get a proper look at that. It is funny how people get excited by different things. I understand we need money to pay for things (although bartering at markets is much more fun, I once got a pig in exchange for two papayas). And treasure is obviously made from precious metals and jewels and gems and is worth a lot of money. So someone getting the treasure could sell it and be very rich. But having lots of money doesn't seem so great to me. It buys you massive houses that you then fill with things that you can't use because you don't have enough time in the day or because you only bought them to fill up space and you don't want them really anyway. Or it buys you nice holidays and butlers and expensive cars that go really, really fast. But you can't drive cars too fast on the roads or you break the law, and butlers are just other people being in your life which would be irritating, and holidays are nice, but you end up going back to where you started from so why didn't you just stay there anyway. My biscuit box treasures aren't worth money. As well as photos and stones I have the wrapper of a chocolate bar called *Zaputtski* that I kept because I like the word and how it looks, a stick with my name 'Maisie' burned into it that tells me who I am and how I spell me, a piece of fleece from a sheep I once talked to when I didn't know how to get through a gorse bush, and two feathers from birds I can't name but who kept me awake when we were on the Galapagos Islands. My treasures make me warm in my head and my body. I missed them, and hoped they were safe at Aunt Hetty's house and that the nosy windowsill pigeon hadn't crept in and scarpered with some of them. They were worth much more than money.

I left the parcel on the stone, patted it once with my hand for good luck, and then turned and began my descent back to Josie. It was much, much harder on the way down, partly because my hands were so cold that it was difficult to know how firmly I was clinging on. Once or twice my fingers or feet slipped, and I had a moment of black, bottomless panic, before finding my grip again. Josie was silent, as if willing all of her concentration onto securing my safety, and it must have worked, because soon I felt her firm hands holding my feet, and guiding them down the last few rungs. I stood next to her on the firm stone floor, only the shakiness of my legs and breathing showing how hard the climb had been. But I had made it. I had done something I didn't know I could do before. Knowing this gave me courage that we could make it, that we could find our way out of this whole situation.

We waited until my knees had stopped wiggling back and forth and I'd had a drink of water, and then it was time to move again. We traced our way back down the tunnel to the original chamber. The journey seemed to take less time, perhaps because the route had some signs of familiarity, or perhaps because we'd achieved the first part of our plan. Once we were in the chamber, Josie stopped and whispered.

'We've done well so far. You've done well. But this is where it becomes more difficult; the route won't be as straightforward. There will be twists and turns, left and right, maybe some more crawling, but hopefully no rock falls. You've seen the way we're going on the map. If, and I mean if, we get separated, you know where to aim for.'

'But we won't though, will we?' It was hard enough being down here with Josie. I couldn't bear to think about being here on my own.

'We shouldn't. However, at each turn, I want you to mark the route we take on the wall of the tunnel itself. Use this.'

She handed me a lump of chalk. 'Mark it low, about waist height.'

'But your waist is different.'

'That's okay. Use your waist to guide you, we just want the mark low. We want to be able to use it if we have to, but I don't want to make the route that we've taken too obvious to anyone else.'

It was like a game that we used to play when I was with my parents. On the day we first arrived wherever we'd travelled to, jungle, beach, frozen wasteland or desert, one of us would go ahead and leave a trail for the other to follow. Small signs, like cutting a notch in a tree leaf or tying a branch back against its trunk; a pebble circle in the sand, or a tiny pyramid built out of snow. All of these subtle signs were indications that someone had passed that way, and the follower was on the right trail. Leaving chalk marks on tunnel walls, well, that was a more obvious one than usual. I knew that I would have to take care, have to make sure that I didn't make the chalk marks stand out too much to unwanted eyes.

I nodded my understanding at her. We turned our backs on the left-hand tunnel and entered the right. Almost immediately the way narrowed so much that we had to turn sideways and inch our way through, the rocks protruding threateningly close to my nose. Moving sideways was awkward, and it also meant that we couldn't see where we were going. I heard Josie curse.

'Don't swear. What's wrong?'

'A puddle. Feels like a mini-lake. Try and step over it if you can; you'll reach it in four shuffles.'

But what size shuffles? I inched along warily, not wanting to end up with flooded boots. Luckily, the tunnel had widened just enough for me to crane my head forward, and the reflection of my headlamp caught the gleam of water on the floor. I stretched forwards with my right foot like a ballet dancer only not as elegantly, and just managed to clear it.

'Was it very deep?'

'Pretty. It went midway up my calf, I was lucky that the tunnel is so tight. There was nowhere for me to fall, so at least I didn't twist my ankle. Apart from a squidgy sock and a slight shock, I'm alright.'

The way became a bit easier after that, widening again so that we could move forwards normally. The cold in my hands was beginning to creep up my wrists, into my arms, twisting into me like ivy. Beneath the surface of the earth, the heat struggled to penetrate, and the damp in the mines brought the temperature even lower. I tried to get some warmth into my limbs doing my best gibbon impression, swinging my arms, clenching and unclenching my fists and rubbing my arms. It helped a little. Josie was keeping a good pace going too, probably more out of urgency than cold, but keeping moving meant that I kept as warm as possible. I thought of my yellow beanie hat sitting on the third shelf of my wardrobe back at Aunt Hetty's house. Her house, my room, everything about my life there seemed so far away. Not just miles in distance, but in time, in space. It felt like another world. I'd never had what most people would call a 'normal' childhood. And I knew that the way I thought wasn't always the same as other people. But it was familiar to me, and I'd also begun to become accustomed to being with Aunt Hetty and the way living went with her. But everything was now thrown. I was in a situation like I'd never been in before. Everything had been tipped upside down, topsy-turvy. It was jumbled in such a way now that I didn't know what threads of my life before would come out in the new one that would be created at the end of this. If there would even be one... The only constant thing was me. At least I could find some reassurance that my thinking and my being were the way they always had been.

'Oof.' I walked straight into Josie's back. 'What's the stop for?' I said into her rucksack.

'Rock fall. But it's only small. We'll have to clamber over it though. Keep your wits about you, Maisie, if you walk into me again, I'll have to find a rock to bop you over the head with.' She laughed.

She was joking (I hoped) but it meant I needed to focus on what was. No more thinking about what had been, what could be. Just think about the here and now.

Josie was right, the rock fall was only small, but it still proved difficult to crawl over. The boulders kept shifting and sliding, and I had to test each one before putting my weight on it to make sure that it wouldn't tumble down with me on it. Once we were both over, muddy and sore from the grazes of several stumbles, the tunnel split into three. I took the chalk out of my pocket, now it would come into some use. We went down the middle one and I quickly dashed a mark on the edge, standing up to the wall to check it was waist height. After this first choice, the network of tunnels really began. Every few steps there were more tunnels appearing. I was glad that Josie was map reading; I became so disorientated and felt as though we were going round in circles. The mix of right and left turns we were taking showed me otherwise, however, and I had to trust that Josie knew exactly where she was taking us. I kept my thoughts on making sure each and every turn was clearly marked – our lifeline if we had to make a quick escape the way we had come and map reading proved too cumbersome. Still the only sounds I could hear were our breathing (hard now, for we were moving fast), the drip drip drip of water, and our splat grind stumble footsteps. So we both came to an abrupt halt when a different noise broke in. This time I didn't walk into Josie's rucksack. We stood, silently, waiting to hear if the noise came again. And then it did, with a low, reverberating CLANGGGG.

'Metal on metal,' Josie whispered at me. 'Someone else is down here.'

The noise came again. It was more than noise. It was a shock that travelled all the way through my body, starting in the bit of my bones that isn't bone and is liquid, going through the hard bit, through my muscles and skin and making all of my hairs vibrate like guitar strings. I tensed everything I could and then shook all of me out, trying to get rid of it.

'Could it be Mum and Dad?' If there was a reason for the noise, I might be able to bear it a bit better.

'It could be, but we're not close enough to where I think they are. We've got to keep moving forward. Slower now, and be as quiet as you can. We need to see if we can find out who, or what, is making the noise before we can decide what to do.'

Walking more slowly, I followed her onwards, the 'clangggg' coming regularly now, punctuating every other footstep. It was taking me ages, as after each noise I had to stop, tense and shake myself. I must have looked like I was doing a silly dance, but it wasn't silly, it was so, so painful, and doing it was the only way I could get myself rid of the string twang electric buzz feeling inside. Putting my hands over my ears didn't help much, but I put the straps of my head torch tightly round them, and that made it a bit muffled. I was getting further behind Josie because I couldn't walk as fast, but she didn't notice. After a few more minutes she stopped again, listening, and I caught up. The clanging continued, rhythmically beating.

'I hate hate hate this. It feels like it's all around, I need it to stop.' I whispered to Josie.

'I know, I can't stand it and that means you must really hate it, but there's nothing we can do. It's hard to put a direction on where it's coming from. Plus, the sound seems to travel so well in the tunnels with the echo they create, that it's difficult to know how far away it is. I think we've just got to keep going. Let me know if you get any indication on where the noise is. If you hear anything behind us, anything at all, let me know. Remember, we may not be the only ones down here.'

CHAPTER 15

I kept nervously glancing backwards as we moved slowly on. I found my footsteps began to keep time with the beats of the clanging, and concentrated on the steady counting rhythm of that, trying to not think about the noise and keep any scary thoughts away. We'd just gone over a cross-roads of tunnels, where four of them decided to confusingly interchange, when I heard it. We'd gone into the straight-ahead tunnel, but as we entered it I heard another sound coming from the right-hand passageway. It was in between the clangs, just when I was doing a left foot shake hop. Josie heard it too, and we stopped immediately. It was a voice.

'I wish they'd stop that flipping noise! There's no point in it, and they can't go anywhere. I've had enough of this black pit. I need some daylight again.'

It carried through to us. Low, complaining. A rumble that grew gradually closer. Josie grabbed me, her mouth close to my ear, and hissed, 'Forward! Move! As quick as you can but no running or they'll hear!'

Luckily this tunnel was wide enough for us to freely walk down rather than wiggle. If we'd run, our hiking boots thumping on the rocky floor would have made our presence obvious to anyone remotely close by, but we could walk quickly, trying to avoid kicking loose stones or splashing in puddles.

Trying to move fast, I couldn't get rid of the horrid noise feeling by going tight then shaky. The one voice became two voices, getting louder by the moment, however quickly we tried to get away. The men must have moved into the tunnel behind us, following our every footstep. It was possible, just about possible, that the men were down here for a reason completely unrelated to Dr Gallows, the kidnaps and the treasure. They could be down here because they were historians looking at old and derelict mine workings, or geologists studying the rock formations in the caves. Or even cavers, hunting for underwater caverns to explore. But then I caught some words which left me with no doubt about the reason they were there.

'So when is the great Dr Gallows coming down here, then?' He sounded fed up, sighing at the end. It was the man with the deep gravelly voice who we'd heard first. Gravel is small stones and pebbles. It makes a nice shoofle sound if you run your fingers through it, but if you stomp across gravel it goes chrruncht chrruncht. As a voice, it's all rough and makes you feel on edge like you just want it to be quiet or only shoofly again.

His companion had a voice nearly as deep, but I didn't think he was from England. His words were short and some of them came out a bit wrong, with 'd's sounding like 't's and 'ee's like 'a's, but I wasn't too certain. 'Don't underestimate Dr Gallows. He will be here later today. To collect the goods from the Voyagers. He wants to thank them…personally.'

They both laughed. It was not a bubbly cascading laugh that washed over you, flooding your face with smiles. It was a short, barking laugh; it wasn't joyful, it was hurtful; it had hard and pointy edges, a jagged stone that tore at me inside. My fists clenched as I heard it. I wanted to hurt them for making fun of my family, for hurting my family, for taking them in the first place. I wanted to hurt the men for making me hurt, for making me scared. I was scared of what Dr Gallows' 'thanks' would actually be. Scared that we wouldn't reach my parents in time.

Josie and I were walking fast, nearly running, and I felt sure that the men must hear us, but it appeared that they were oblivious, lost in their conversation as they concentrated on getting up to daylight again. Their voices and their heavy, thumping footsteps grew ever closer, and although the tunnel twisted and turned, I kept looking behind, to check that there was no sign of them.

Suddenly the tunnel forked into two, looking just like the hands of my watch when it's ten to two, or ten minutes past ten.

'Left!' Josie hissed and we darted down the ten-hour-hand tunnel and pressed ourselves tight against the wall. We were both going 'whoof whoof' in our breathing, and then crunching footsteps and conversation were suddenly upon us. What if they were to go left? Where would we go then? They paused. And I heard the rustle of paper unfolding. I still hadn't breathed out and in again; my chest was tight under all my clothes, as if my lungs were filling my body and not leaving any space for my heart. I started letting some of my inside air come out my nose to try and make it feel like I wasn't going to burst.

'Flipping maze, this place,' the man with the gravel voice grumbled. 'Just glad we've got this map, otherwise I think we'd never get in and out safely. Anyway, it's right.'

Did he mean right the opposite of left, or right the opposite of wrong? I still didn't know if they would come down our tunnel. I heard feet beginning to scuff. I took a tiny sip of air as quiet as I could in case the slightest sound caught their attention.

'Wait.' This time it was the strange-speaking man. 'You said it was right?'

'Yes. Come on.'

'Then why are there footprints leading to the left?'

'Probably because I headed that way the other time I was down here, by accident or something.'

'With feet that small? I don't think so. Something else is going on here.'

Josie suddenly turned to me. 'Go!' she whispered urgently. 'Maisie, you've got to go. Follow this tunnel down a little way further. They'll find me, but then you can get away. They won't think there are two of us. If we both get caught there's no hope. You know the map. Come and find us. Come and get us. I know you can do it.'

I had no time to think. I had no time to question. I just had to follow Josie's instructions. I gave her hand a tight squeeze and ran. It didn't matter about noise. Not for the moment. I could run until they found Josie and then I would have to stop. Not knowing how long I had, I wanted to get as far away as possible. Just in case they did decide to come searching...

I could hear something behind. I could hear muffled grunts and I imagined pushes and shoves. The clanging had stopped and there were no cries; no words from Josie either. Maybe she'd decided that silence was best – to submit, but say nothing rather than fight. Then the scuffling stopped. I stopped too.

'Well...that's another one for the pile...' It was strange-speaking man.

'Do you think she's part of them?' Gravel voice was puffing hard.

'There's no other reason for her to be down here. On her own in a tin mine in Cornwall? No, she's got to be part of this somehow. We'll let Dr Gallows figure it out. Come on, let's dump her with the others and then get on out of here.'

Two sets of footsteps began, accompanied by the sound of a heavy object being dragged along the floor. I knew the sound because I'd heard one like it before. Several months ago I'd developed an interest in Hannibal and his elephants and the long explorations they'd gone on, hundreds of years ago. I liked the idea of exploring with elephants. They'd carry a bit more for you than donkeys or camels. Anyway, I was pretending to be an elephant going up a mountain, and was pulling Aunt Hetty's compost bag up the garden path (at least I was until it split open and compost went everywhere). It made the same dragging schhhhhhh noise as this. This noise wouldn't be compost bags though, it must be Josie. If she was being dragged, that meant she couldn't walk. And she hadn't cried out so they must have knocked her unconscious. The idea of being unconscious was strange. I didn't mind going to sleep at night like you're supposed to do, but I didn't want to be suddenly asleep when I was supposed to be awake. At least if Josie was unconscious she wasn't awake to experience all of the horrible events. But what if she wasn't just unconscious? What if she…? I shut my eyes and shook my head, chasing away the terrible thought. I felt like I'd seen purple colours everywhere, like someone had done lots of tickly touching all over my skin, like I had no idea who or where I was or what was going on. I had to concentrate to stop myself breathing quicker and quicker, had to count numbers again, to focus, to calm myself down and let my fears subside. Counting has an absolute order. It is what it is, and it never changes (even if you put halves and quarters and eighths in between, it still goes up in the same way). I can trust counting, and if I can trust that, I can start to trust other things again. I couldn't make all of my fears go away, but I did force myself to think about now and not on what might be.

So, now, what was I going to do next? I wanted to follow the men. I knew that they would lead me straight to my parents, and that was where I wanted to go more than anything else. But I knew that if I followed them, I would end up trapped. There might not be any hiding places to stop them from seeing me, and even if I hit them really, really hard, I didn't think I'd actually manage to overpower them on my own. So following them was out of the question. But what if I waited in this tunnel until they came back? They said they needed to go down the right tunnel to get to the surface, so they wouldn't need to come down mine. Once I'd heard them go that way, they would definitely be gone for a while. And then I could revert to Josie's and my original plan and use the mine map to find my parents' location. As the clumping of feet and the horrible sound of dragging faded into distant echoes, I risked switching on my torch. Pulling out the mine plan from my pocket, I studied it closely. Tracking the network of lines with my finger, I could work out where we'd been, and also the passageway I must now be in. Tracing back, I worked out where we'd been aiming for. The old shaft. It wasn't too far. Good. That would mean I wouldn't have to wait for long.

It was cold. So, so cold down here. Standing still, my toes grew numb and then gradually the numb began seeping upwards, spreading from my toes to my feet, my fingers to my arms. Numb is black, deep dark black. When my torch was off, there was no light, nothing, I couldn't even see my hand when I put it next to my eye. The numb and cold was that blackness but inside me. I tried wiggling my toes in my socks, to get some feeling back and clapped my hands together (as silently as possible) before tucking them deep into my armpits and trying to find some warmth there.

I'd been in some cold places before. It's funny but the desert at night time can be colder than a snowy country. When I'd been in these places though, I'd had thick fleecy clothes and fires that made me hot again. Most of the time I learned different survival skills just by watching people, but I do remember my mum once saying to me, 'When you've got a fire that's growing cold, put some more fuel on. If your body's getting chilled, give it some food. You need fuel for warmth.' I remembered it because I liked the idea of being a fire, of being magic flames that could be red and orange and blue and green. Food. That would help to make me warm. What I really wanted was a toasty hot mug of chocolate. Steaming hot! Made properly with milk and grated chocolate, whisked until a thick froth floated on the top and gave me a moustache as I drank. Despite her other cooking disasters, Aunt

Hetty made the best hot chocolate like that. It was an Aunt Hetty hug in a mug, tight and squeezing, making everything seem better. I sighed. Was it really only a few days since I'd sat in the kitchen after art class? It felt like another world.

Moving around and travelling so much, I got used to changing places. One week I could be listening to the lonely call of a Tibetan yak in the Himalayan mountains (it goes 'Moaaaaaaaaahw'), and the next I could be chasing away a llama who'd just spat at me as I tried to stroke its nose during a street market in Peru. But people had always been constant. I knew, wherever I was, I could look over my shoulder and see a face I could rely on. Someone who could translate for me when my grasp of a language got no further than 'Hallo, I'm Maisie. How are you?' Someone who could dig me out of a snowdrift when I got too enthusiastic building igloos and it all collapsed on top of me. Someone who would put a light in my tent each night for protection and comfort. Someone who let me ask questions again and again so I could hear the answer (I just liked the sound of the words 'baba ghanoush' even though I didn't like the sticky dip made from purple aubergines). Someone who explained words to me when I got confused by double meanings. Someone who gave me time to be me. Mum and Dad knew who I was. Josie understood lots about me. And Aunt Hetty was getting to know me too.

For the last few days, I felt like I'd been alone. That was something so alien to me. Not the actual being alone (I was more than used to my own company) – but there being no one else there somewhere along the way. There being no one I could go and talk to about what I'd been doing afterwards. There being no one making comforting 'other people in the house' noises. Right now, I knew that just a short distance away were the people I loved, and the people who knew me better than anyone. I so, so wanted to run to be with them, to get captured anyway because it would mean I could be with them. But I knew I couldn't. I had to become someone on a mission, become a soldier again. Become someone who could think about making it better for everyone, not just making it better for me. To start with, I had to take care of myself on my own for just a little bit longer. And right now that meant eating something.

I scrabbled in the side pocket of my rucksack, looking for the supplies Josie had stashed there. There was (yet another) cereal bar with 'oats, raisins, cranberries and chocolate chunks'. I'd had quite a lot of them recently, and wouldn't have minded something different. Cereal bars are made by machines and get packaged and sent through the factory on conveyor belts. There are thousands and thousands of them all looking the same. When you eat them, they all taste the same. I don't mind knowing what to expect, but the same thing over and over can be tiring if you don't want it. This cereal bar didn't look too much like hamster food though and was definitely the thing to give me some energy. A soldier would eat it, and I was a soldier at the moment. There were also two toffees nestling beneath it and I tucked them into the pocket of my trousers to be used at a later emergency. The bar was sweet, like the colour of flames, and although not quite the hot chocolate I had been dreaming of, did actually help me to start feeling warmer.

I was feeling slightly better – my skin wasn't as bumpy and I'd stopped shivering. I could sort of imagine my fingers feeling warmer. They were more dark grey than pitch black feeling now. Then I heard the sound of footsteps again. This time they were moving faster, and I guessed that the men were hurrying to get out of the tunnels, desperate for some daylight. I heard the footsteps get louder and then fade again. They must have walked off down the right fork now. I left it another few minutes to be sure that they weren't returning, and then I began to walk again. Round and round went the thoughts in my head but my feet just kept on moving forwards. I took a step at a time, cautiously listening but knowing that my mission had properly started now, and I needed to advance. I had to get to my family, my friends, before the men came back. Naming the men Strange-speaking man and Gravel voice made the fear I had of them more manageable. It was less easy to be terrified of something that had a silly name.

My head was spinning skywards but my feet were moving forwards and all the time I followed my map along the dark and entwining tunnels. My head torch pointing down at the map made my feet have huge long shadows, but there was no real shadow of the rest of me. I had to keep touching my arms and my chest and face to check I was there. I kept following the route when suddenly the gap, the distance to the cage area where Josie and I had always been heading for, was nearly underneath my grimy, grey and dirt-smudged fingertip. Just a few more metres. My pace quickened. I couldn't help it. I knew I shouldn't just throw away my caution and run, but my footsteps went faster all the same. I couldn't hear anything but the sound of my feet and my breathing. But silence didn't mean they weren't there. Did it? They had to be there. They had to! Left... right...one more turning...and then my feet wouldn't obey my head and they ran. I had to know if my family were there. I rounded the last corner before the shaft and caught my foot. At the speed I was running, I sprawled headfirst along the floor, scraping my knees and hands and hitting my chin so that I literally saw stars. Shooting white lights flew across my eyes. I lay, spread-eagled, stunned and soon to be very sore. Landing on my chest and tummy had literally oomphed all of the breath from me, and I had nothing left to make a sound with.

'Maisie?'

CHAPTER 16

When I was five years and three months old, I was in Morocco. My parents had been travelling with some desert nomads to see how they survived out in the sandy wilderness. After a few weeks in the desert we'd returned to the city of Marrakesh. The plan was to spend a day visiting markets, bartering for sweet and sticky dates and beautiful handmade fabrics – a welcome reprieve after sand, sun and sulky camels. We were at a stall displaying oil lamps, the multicoloured glass winking, flashing, mesmerising in the sunlight. I was entranced, captivated. I felt like I was standing in the middle of a rainbow and couldn't bear to move out and let the colours leave me.

I didn't notice Mum and Dad move on. When I finally turned around, they weren't there. There was no one and nothing familiar, just hustle and bustle, the chatter, shouting, sounds and smells of a thousand unfamiliar people. I froze, my head turning left and right, up and down, looking all around. My feet wouldn't, couldn't, move. Should I go and look for them? Should I stay? What if I went and they came back? What if I stayed and they didn't know how to return? I didn't know where to go or what to do. Biting my lip, I concentrated very hard, trying to make the tears go back into my eyes and stop tickling my cheeks. I felt like the most minuscule insect in sky high grass, the world looming above. The market had seemed so bright and happy moments before, but it now crowded threateningly around me. And then suddenly I heard it. Somehow, amongst the bleating of goats, the traders' cries, I heard her voice calling.

'Maisie? Maisie?'

It was tinged with panic. The ice-blue of fear raising her words so her voice was higher sounding than normal. But I heard the words behind me, and my feet came alive and I turned to face my mum and flung myself into her arms.

My arms and legs were sprawled out in the shape of a parachute jumper. Lying on the cold stone floor of a long-disused tin mine, I heard that voice again. This time, the ice-blue was gone from her voice. It was scared, tentative, but surrounded by the glowing hues of a thousand rainbows.

'Mum?' As I spoke, I hauled myself up, focusing only on the words I heard.

My torch had been flung from my head when I fell, but somehow it refused to break, and the light cast a dim glow over the tunnel. It pointed into more blackness. I reached out and circled it around. I couldn't work out the direction where the voice was. The echoes of it bounced off the walls filling my ears with words upon words all calling 'Maisie, Maisie, Maisie.' The torchlight was dim and pale, but then it shone on something and I felt as though my world had suddenly been illuminated by a million candles.

Behind a metal cage were the faces of Mum, Dad, Aunt Hetty and Palo. I could see their eyes, all looking at me. For once, it didn't make me feel like they were looking into my brain; it made me feel that I was something important to be seen. And again I heard the voice.

'Maisie!' It was echoed this time by other real voices, not just echoes.

'Mum, Dad, Aunt Hetty!' I propelled myself across to them and clung to the bars, my hands entwined with all of theirs. None of us could speak for a moment. And when I looked up I saw tears streaming down their faces, and felt that mine was the same. I sometimes cry when I'm sad, but I don't usually cry when I'm happy. It was as though the weeks and months of pain of being apart, and fear for each other's safety, all bubbled over from the inside and came flowing outside through the tears on our cheeks. I gave a huge sniff and then Dad spoke.

'We have to act. Now. And fast.'

His voice brought us back to reality and to the gravity of the present situation. Although we were all there together, they were still locked on one side, and I was on the other.

Shining the torch around, I could see that they were in one of the old cages that were used to take men up and down the mine from the surface, like we had thought. The cage door was padlocked shut. I had a sudden mad moment where I wondered if I could get the pulley system working and lift the cage to the surface. But a closer look at the chains, wheels and cogs showed that they were rusted and broken beyond quick repair. There was a long metal ladder though that stretched up the shaft, reaching up to the daylight and fresh air above. Looking up, I could see far above my head there was another grille covering the shaft, but maybe once we got to it, we could find some way of getting it open. It was either that or we had to go all the way back through the tunnels, the way Josie and I had come.

I looked at Dad.

'Up the shaft's the only way,' he said as if reading my mind and answering my question.

'How did you…'

'I saw you looking.'

I felt a bit of relief, knowing he hadn't actually seen my thoughts.

'But before the shaft, we've got to get out of this cage.'

'How?' I didn't want to seem pathetic, but at the same time, had no idea of how we were supposed to get out of the situation.

'We use Dr Gallows. Is the treasure in the recess up a tunnel wall?' I nodded. 'Good, Josie's followed the instructions. Well, when Dr Gallows comes down, we tell him where it is and he lets us go.'

'But how do you know he won't trick us?'

'The likelihood is that he'll try. But I think, ultimately, Dr Gallows is motivated by greed more than revenge. He'll want to take the treasure and run.'

'But what about his men? But...'

'But, but, but,' my dad broke in. 'Buts are for?'

'Billygoats. Yes, Dad, I know.' I inwardly groaned at his old, worn-out sayings, but, deep down, part of me was secretly overjoyed at hearing something so predictable and comfortingly familiar again.

A moan emerged from the back of the cage and I swung the light there, startled. Palo was crouched by an unmoving lump, huddled in the far corner.

'Josie?' I hadn't thought about it at the time, but when I'd seen all of the faces behind the cage, one was missing. I'd been so fixed on the faces of my parents, I hadn't realised that Josie wasn't there.

'She's coming round...I think.' Palo said. He stumbled over his words – usually he was so clear and determined. He didn't sound like he believed what he was saying.

I felt a tight knot in my stomach, twisting, clenching my insides.

'We must get out of here soon. She needs a doctor.' Palo was wiping Josie's face with some water. 'It's her head. I can't tell how hard she hit it or what injury she's got.' Palo was the expedition's regular medic. He was a qualified army nurse. If he didn't know how badly she was hurt, it meant that it was serious.

'Listen to me now, Maisie.' My dad's voice became quiet and his words were quick.

I turned to him.

'You have to go – you have to hide. If Dr Gallows comes and sees you here, it will confuse him. He won't be expecting it and it will just make him panic. If he panics...well, that just puts us all in more danger.'

I nodded, hating what he was saying, but understanding.

Mum spoke next, they'd obviously worked out a plan. I supposed they'd had enough time to think things over, sitting down there in the darkness. She sounded like she was just telling me to go and wash my face, or clean the dishes. It was as though this was just another job that needed to be done. 'You need to go, just a short way away, but go and hide. Make sure that you can still hear us, so that you know what's going on, and stay hidden. Once Dr Gallows comes, and hopefully goes, and we're free, then you can either meet up with us again and we'll get out of here together...'

'Or if we're escorted out, you can go back through the tunnels and out the way you came. Think you'd be able to do that?' The last bit came from Aunt Hetty. Surprisingly for someone who didn't usually spend most of their time in strange, dangerous places, she sounded like Mum, all calm and normal. Perhaps she was more like Mum and Dad than I thought. I nodded at her, trying to be like them, show that I could be calm and ordered too.

Dad carried on. 'And then we'll meet at the cove, where our tent is. If things don't go to plan, well, at least you'll still be free and able to go and get help. If something goes wrong, then, Maisie, you must get help this time. No being a hero warrior on your own. You have to go and get help.' Dad spoke with such forcefulness. It was his 'I need you to listen to me' serious voice; the one he used when he was teaching me about poisonous snakes, or how to collect drinking water if I got lost in a jungle. When he used that voice I knew it could be deadly if I didn't listen to his guidance.

'But it shouldn't come to that?' I didn't like the idea of deadly, it was too scary.

'No...' his answer hung, the o o o echoing like a bell.

I looked at his face, saw the soft brown eyes, just like mine, and drew strength from that. If I had Dad's eyes, I could be strong like him too. Our hands knotted tightly together, mine, Mum's, Dad's and Aunt Hetty's, and then I turned and limped away from them, back into the tunnel system. Walking away from the people I loved, from the people I'd been hurting so desperately for, was one of the hardest things I've ever had to do. But I knew that they were right, that by walking away I was giving us the best chance of getting back together again.

I counted my paces and when I got to a hundred steps, I stopped. The tunnel was about to divide into two anyway, so staying where I was seemed the best plan. I hunkered down. Hunker is a word that always makes me think of hamsters and chipmunks, but it just means crouching. I wrapped my arms around my legs and I suppose I must have looked like some small, balled up creature. I examined my knees that were stinging from when I fell. They were grazed and bleeding, and my palms looked the same. I got out some tissues from my rucksack and soaked them in water from my bottle, then I dabbed at the grit as best I could, trying to get the dirt out. I couldn't help squeaking in pain, making me sound like a small animal as well as looking like one. They weren't clean, but I didn't want to risk wasting any more water so I pulled out my handkerchief and tied it around the worst grazed knee, hoping to keep it from getting any dirtier at least. Sore, tired, cold and alone, I decided it was definitely time for one of the toffees I'd been saving. Unwrapping it, I popped it in my mouth. Sweet flavours are familiar, you can find sugary food wherever you go, whether it's toffee in England, mangos in Pakistan, honey in Greece or sugar cane in Jamaica. Sucking on the sweetness gave me a small amount of comfort. Resisting the temptation to chew, I sucked away until the very last scrap was gone and, as I swallowed, I heard footsteps and voices. They were muffled at first, but then more distinct. I recognised them. It was Short Words, Gravel and Dr Gallows. I stood up silently and took three silent steps forward, trying to make my ears hear any words they said.

The voices were loud and sounded much more relaxed than I felt; they were even laughing a bit. But then they were nearly at the conclusion of their whole plan. They were about to get the treasure that they'd been waiting for. They had no reason to be unhappy.

The footsteps stopped. They must have reached where they were going. The cage.

'Well. How nice to see you all again. And Josie is it? Well, Josie, it's very nice to meet you too. Sorry about your head, but accidents do so frequently happen in these dangerous tunnels...rock falls...cave-ins...you know how it is.' Dr Gallows sounded the same as when he'd come to Aunt Hetty's house – smooth and confident. He believed he was supremely in control.

'And now it's time. You are all here. There is no one left; no one else you can call on. And who would hear you anyway?' All of the men laughed. It clashed like lots of saucepans falling on a floor and I put my hands on my ears. But then I couldn't hear the conversation. I didn't know what to do. I couldn't bear the sound, but I had to know what was going on. I remembered Dad's eyes, Dad's strength, and took my hands away. The echoes of laughter were quieter now.

'So...the hoard...where is it?' Dr Gallows was talking.

'You are right.' My dad spoke. 'There is no one left. We don't want to do this. We think you, your people, what you are doing here is disgusting. You think nothing of the people that have been, the way life was lived, the way lives are lived now. You just want to take all that you can, take and take and take...'

'Oh, Gerald, Gerald. Save your words. You just sound pathetic like a character in a bad film. If all you're going to do is lecture me on the niceties of life, then save your breath. Because if you continue, that breath will be your last.' His voice had changed from light and high pitched to have a dark, deep edge. It was a voice that meant what it said.

'Alright.' Mum took over. 'We've had enough. We'll tell you where it is. But then you need to let us go.'

'I will let you go when I have it; even you should be able to work that out. There is no benefit for me in keeping you here, or even killing you. Who knows what more delights you might uncover for me in future years? Tell me where this hoard is and I will send the men to get it. Once they return, if everything is in order, then I will let you go. The map is here. Show me the location.'

There was silence for a few moments and I wondered what was happening.

'Right, right. Luis and Pete, go. Take this, and find it. I will stay here.'

Footsteps led off. They must have shown Dr Gallows the location on the map.

'Well, well! Isn't this cosy?' Dr Gallows sounded much friendlier again, his pleasing nature returned now that he was getting what he wanted.

There was a low groan, which I presumed was Josie trying to come round. It was a horrible sound to hear, but at least it meant she was still alive.

The noise obviously spurred Dr Gallows on. I heard his footsteps quicken as he paced around, and I imagined his arms gesticulating enthusiastically as he spoke emphatically. It was as though he was on a stage performing, and I supposed that he did have an audience of sorts, although they weren't there by choice.

'You see, the thing is, all of this…this palaver. This kidnapping, trickery, chasing around England, and skulking about in disused tunnels only fit for mice… it will all have been pointless. I've ended up with your notes, the plans and maps for the source of the treasure. Plus the treasure itself.'

He was wrong; there weren't any mice in the tunnels. And the chasing around England was because we were trying to get away from him. He started it, but was making it sound like everything was our fault.

'And you. Well, I presume that you will have been inconvenienced if not a little traumatised by all this. You have behaved very selfishly. If you had only given me what I asked for, no one would have had to suffer at all.'

Mum and Dad had to teach me that what I wanted wasn't always what was best, or what other people wanted. They taught me that I sometimes had to compromise or put other people first, because then everyone would be happier. It didn't sound like anyone had taught that to Dr Gallows. He was so self-centred. I don't think anyone knew what to say, but then Dad spoke.

'You know full well why we wouldn't just hand things over. This isn't about wealth and gems and jewels. This is history and life. We want to preserve the objects and the memories of history. You just take, and don't think about the space you've left behind. Fine. You've got the treasure. But what next? Why continue on this path?' He spoke passionately, in the voice he used when teaching me about countries, about people. When he spoke like that, I got all interested, all enthusiastic about his words and what he might tell me next. It didn't do that to Dr Gallows.

'Because both you and I know that where the treasure came from, there's a whole lot more.' Dr Gallows continued. 'Why should I settle for this? Maybe I would have once. But not now. Not now I've seen what else there could be, how very small this hoard is in comparison. And especially not now I've gone to all this trouble.' He made his voice louder on the last three words.

'We'll follow you.' It was Palo who spoke, quiet but sure. 'We'll follow you. As far as you go, we'll be behind.'

Dr Gallows laughed. 'Clichés. That's all. You're as good as saying "You won't get away with this!" But I will. I already have. The plans you had, well, they're all now in my possession. So even if you made it as far as the Caribbean, you would have to guess what journey to make next. And I think that, even as keen on exploring as you are, you would not spend the rest of your life hopping from one island to another just to try to find me. So I have all of the maps, your book of notes and, of course, the bundle of the papers that Josie so kindly handed over when my men encountered her. Papers filled with directions and diagrams. But I tell you what – when I've got there, when I've found what I'm looking for and made my fortune, I'll let you know. I'll…send you a postcard. How does that sound? Then you can join in the celebrations with me!' He laughed, but he laughed on his own.

No one else said anything. Dr Gallows' desire and greed meant he thought about nothing but himself. You couldn't reason with someone with an ego that large. I'd nearly lost concentration when he was talking; there were too many words for me to focus. My thoughts were whirling, rapidly trying to process everything he was saying. Some bits I remembered – more treasure? The Caribbean? And what were the maps he was talking about? As always, I felt I had far too many questions and far too few answers. I knew Josie would never have just handed the notes over; they must have gone through her rucksack when she was captured. I thought that the book was one of Dad's most treasured possessions. It was refillable, and he kept it for making all of his most important notes in. He always kept it in the left back pocket of his shorts, desert trousers, or snow pants. In being captured by Dr Gallows, he must have had to hand it over. This loss would be greater for him than any other. He'd managed to hang on to the book while dangling upside down from a creeper vine above an anaconda-infested river and while being charged by an irritated bull elephant who'd got frustrated when Dad had tried to get too close to his breakfast. To have the notebook taken from him by such a detestable man as Dr Gallows was nearly unthinkable. And the fact that its current contents were obviously so valuable made it all the worse. I fumed, silently, feeling my fingers tighten and my face get hard. If nothing else, even if he couldn't be stopped from escaping, we had to get that notebook back. It represented all that my parents spent their life working for. But how could we do it?

Dr Gallows continued to laugh in the silence. Through his laughter I could hear the footsteps of the others returning.

'Well?' His voice was eager with anticipation and excitement.

'Here. Luis found it. Just where they'd marked.' The deep voice spoke; Pete must be Gravel.

There was a distant rustle. And then silence. I bit my lip. Would he believe in it? Was Josie's contact really as good as she said? Was Dr Gallows really going to fall for it?

'Finally, finally.' There was a pause. 'This was worth any amount of time grovelling around down here in the dark. Take a look…it will be the last time. Try and remember the brightness, the shimmering beauty. Because memories will be all that you have.'

I wished I could see it. I'd never seen real treasure (even fake real treasure). Aunt Hetty took me to a big building in a city where there were hundreds of objects from history. She told me it was a museum, a collection of things from long ago lives. There were lots of stone statues, pots that were broken into pieces and dirty old coins that looked like squashed bottle tops. It was interesting, but not treasure. The only gold thing was a coffin from a mummy that had been found in a pyramid in Egypt. I wasn't too sure about the coffin. It seemed a bit of a waste to have something so beautiful that you wouldn't even see because you were dead. I couldn't be sure that there wasn't still a body inside it, and the eyes painted on the coffin seemed to follow me around as I moved. Aunt Hetty and I had quickly gone back to the broken pots, which seemed a lot safer. I stopped thinking about mummies; it was making me feel nervous.

'You've got it. Now let us go.' Dad sounded tired, defeated. I didn't know if he was really feeling that way, or was putting it on in an effort to convince Dr Gallows. Either way, I just wanted to put my arms around him. Holding his hand had been a small comfort, but a hug with my dad was like nothing else, he could hug tighter than anyone or anything (apart from a boa constrictor, and I didn't want a hug from one of those, that would be just too squeezy). A Dad hug was another joy that would have to wait for the moment though.

'Pete, pack this back up while I unlock the door.' Dr Gallows gave orders. 'You expected me to kill you perhaps? I am no killer, no murderer. I have not harmed anyone…your unconscious friend in the corner there injured herself because she was foolish enough to get in my way. That is her fault. But I am not going to kill you. That serves me no purpose, and as I said, I fully expect to be in touch with you again, regarding any of your future finds. We could even find ourselves together again in a situation like this…but that is your choice. You need never be locked up again, never imprisoned, if you only follow my requests.' He sighed. 'Look, I'm tired of talking, it's serving me no purpose.' Good, I was tired of him talking too. It was all a bit much. 'I want you to go with Pete and Luis to the cove, they will lead you out of the tunnels and leave you there.'

There was a solid-sounding clank, and a scronching sound as metal scraped along stone. Footsteps. I held my breath. I knew people didn't always mean what they said. I didn't trust Dr Gallows, would he really let them go? It occurred to me that I had made no plans, given no thought to what would have happened if he had decided to hurt them. Even if I'd gone into SAS soldier mode I could have done very, very little. I had no weapons. There was a spoon in my pack, but spoons aren't very sharp. I still would have hurtled myself at Dr Gallows though, all fingernails, fists and teeth, biting and clawing at him. I would have done my very own impression of a fighting possum, fighting not for my survival, but for the survival of those I loved. But I was lucky. Lucky, lucky, lucky that I was not even going to have to consider that.

'I wish I could...' Mum began to speak, but then trailed off.

'Could what? Take the gold off me? Stop me?' Another small laugh came from Dr Gallows' sneaky lips. 'You can do none of that. Just thank me, for sparing you. And now I will say goodbye to you all apart from Henrietta here.'

'What? Why?' Aunt Hetty sounded stunned. 'What can I do?'

'You are the best security I could have. I can't run the risk that somehow Margaret and Gerald will get away from Luis and Pete. For all I know, they could have become karate experts after their recent time in Japan. I have planned everything so perfectly and carefully up to now, and am not going to have it all crumble around me at the last moment. So go on, shoo. You too. If she can't walk, you'll have to carry her.'

He must have been talking to Palo and Josie at the end. I heard Palo grunt and a dragging noise as he pulled and hauled Josie out.

'Off. Go, now. And once I am certain that you are left in the cove, Pete and Luis have met up with me, and that you have not divulged any of this to the security services or police, then I will let her go. It'll only be a few days. Just so that I can get away and be sure that I am safe.'

'Go.' Aunt Hetty spoke. Her voice was quiet, low, but solid. 'You have to. Go now. I will be with you soon.'

There was nothing more to be said. I heard the sound of footsteps drawing closer, and then beginning to fade as they rounded a corner and followed the tunnel away from me, away from the cage, away from Dr Gallows and back towards the surface.

CHAPTER 17

I was left in a dilemma. Did I follow them down the tunnels towards safety? If Pete and Luis heard me following, this could create a problem, but there would be enough of us to probably overpower them. I so, so wanted to go and started to turn in that direction. Having been so close to my parents only to hear them getting physically further away with every step, gave me this sharp bright pain inside. Like when you look at a bright light and it hurts your eyes, that's how it was in my chest. And there was Josie, my person who knew me, who understood my head. I wanted to make sure that she was safe, that she wasn't seriously hurt.

There was also Aunt Hetty. She wasn't my mum, but she made me feel like my mum did. She was different, slightly more practical and homely; she reminded me to have a bath rather than encouraging me to eat witchety grubs, or taught me how to iron shirts instead of how to hang them on tree branches to dry. But she was someone who I had grown to rely on, someone who let me be me. I couldn't leave her on her own. And maybe, just maybe, I could stop Dr Gallows taking her away.

I turned back and began to move. Slowly, surely, one footstep at a time. My sore knees said 'hurt, hurt, hurt' at me, but I ignored them, balling my hands into fists, drawing strength from that.

'I understand why you're taking me.' Aunt Hetty sounded a little less secure now she was alone.

'I expected that you would. And let's just make one thing clear: it is of no benefit for me to kill you. You are an important person within the governmental science world, and to be honest, although your death would cause me absolutely no sadness whatsoever, I have no desire to suffer the consequences of it if I should ever get caught. I fully expect to be able to talk or barter my way out of any theft charges, should they ever arise. But murder? That is a harder one. So your life is in no danger. But. And this is a big but. There are many things that I could do to you that would not result in your death, but would cause you a lot of pain. Not just now, but as a permanent fixture. And don't forget, I can cause you pain, but I can also cause pain to those you love and care for. Including children. That niece of yours is not exempt.

So, if you have any wild ideas about escaping, pause for a moment and ask yourself if it's really worth it.'

That niece was me. I didn't want him to cause me pain but I had to make sure Aunt Hetty was safe. I kept moving closer.

'Right, right. Onwards and upwards. Literally. We are going to climb this ladder to the surface. You are going to go first, and I will follow right behind.'

I had to move. And fast. When you watch action films, like James Bond and Indiana Jones, when they meet the bad guys and have to fight suddenly, you can see that they haven't thought anything through. They're just acting in the first way they thought of, the best way they've been trained how to survive, or protect the people they're looking after. Everything I did next was just action. I didn't think. I couldn't think. I just followed every action film Aunt Hetty had ever shown me, every adventure book I'd ever read. I forgot I was Maisie, forgot I was a person. I just became what I was doing. Just did what I thought I had to. It's scary that your head can forget yourself, that your head can get lost in a moment and you don't even realise it.

Their footsteps began to thunk on the rungs of the ladder and I guessed they must be climbing. I rounded the corner and saw the empty cage, the door open, filled with shadows not people. And on the ladder were two figures reaching, climbing, moving steadily upwards. I had to follow. As silently as I could I began to climb. I had to hope with every bit of me that Dr Gallows would not look back down. If he did, then I would be discovered. And who knew what the consequence of that would be.

I was lucky. Although he was tall and skinny, Dr Gallows was not fit, and he wheezed like an old donkey as he hauled himself upwards, completely obscuring any sounds that I made. It was a long climb. I tried to concentrate on numbers again, counting the rungs, focusing on anything other than the situation I was in. The metal rungs were cold and hard on my hands, I could feel gritty rust under my fingertips. Was the ladder falling apart under my hands? Would it collapse before I got to the top? I looked down; it would be a very long way to fall. I could feel each flake of rust, I could feel every one. When my first tooth got wobbly, Mum told me that it would soon wobble out and I'd have a space for a bit, and then a new one would grow in its place. When it actually wobbled out (in the middle of eating a frozen banana), I was a bit surprised to suddenly hold my tiny tooth in my hand. It looked like a little pebble, it didn't look like something that chomped on fruit and nuts and bread. I stuck my tongue in the gap where the tooth had once been. It was like a cavern in my mouth and I screamed. I couldn't stop screaming. I felt a huge hole, much bigger than my little tooth and didn't know what had happened. Mum got me to calm down and then took me to the nearest bucket of water. She told me to look in it at my face and open my mouth. I refused, because I didn't want to see my teeth looking all different; I didn't want to see my face not looking like me. But eventually she convinced me to, and she was right, it was a tiny space; it was only a little place where my tooth had sat. But my tongue still told me it was huge. I had to keep running back to the bucket to check. By the time my next tooth fell out, I was ready for what to expect. It taught me that what I felt, and what was real, wasn't always the same. Here, although each flake of rust felt like a big chunk of metal, it was really very tiny. I talked to myself in my head, 'The ladder won't collapse, you will be okay. Climb, Maisie, climb.'

I got to 158, then 159 and suddenly we stopped. I was eight rungs below Dr Gallows. The bottom of his boots were rubber black and had wavy lines on them. I could read the number thirteen, he must have big feet, my shoes only had the number three on them. The shaft was brighter here, and I could make out the murky brown colour of the walls. Sunlight was drifting down; we must be nearing the surface.

'I can't open the grille.' Aunt Hetty's voice travelled down to my ears.

'Push hard. It's stiff but you can push it up and out.' Dr Gallows huffed in between each word. If I was breathing that hard, I would have needed a lie down, let alone a brief break in the climb. Would he even get to the top?

I held myself as flat as possible against the ladder, holding on and waiting. I looked up. Dr Gallows' big, black boots looked like they could crush my fingers without a moment's thought. I traced the wavy line pattern with my eyes, getting lost in the ups and downs. But something flicking in the corner of my eye made me stop. One of his boots had a lace undone. Again, without really thinking, I moved up four rungs and stretched. My fingers caught the dangling bootlace, gently tying it, double knotting it, triple knotting it around the metal slat of ladder. That ought to delay him, but what now?

There was a rasping screech as the grille finally opened.

'Move.' Dr Gallows gave instructions. 'And there's nowhere to run when you get out, so don't try to go anywhere. Chasing after you would be easy but tedious, and it's probably better that you avoid irritating me in the first place.'

Aunt Hetty's feet climbed up. Then Dr Gallows tried to move. And couldn't. He tugged at his boot, obviously thinking it was stuck a little. But when it wouldn't move, he swore loudly and looked down.

'What the...?' he saw the lace knotted to the rung. And then he looked further, past the boot, and saw my face, peering up at him out of the gloom.

'You!'

That one word was all he could utter. Spluttering, he became incoherent with rage as he kicked his foot against the ladder trying to free it.

'How could you...? Why...? What...?'

I said nothing, but backed down a few steps. His eyes were pure fury, dark and whirling with flecks of light burning inside. They spat embers at me, trying to sear me with their anger. I waited, shaking. I had no idea what to do next. And then I realised that he was stuck. He was carrying the package in one hand, and so couldn't take his other hand off the side of the ladder in order to reach down and untie the lace. But he couldn't hand the package up to Aunt Hetty to hold, or he would lose any power he had over her. Swearing furiously with some wonderful new words I'd never heard before (I saved them to say to myself later), he stuffed the corner of the package into his mouth and, holding on with his left hand, he reached down and started scrabbling frantically at his boot. I looked up past him and could see the shadow of Aunt Hetty near the opening. She wasn't moving, trying to assess what was going on. Perhaps she couldn't see, perhaps she was paralysed with fear herself, uncertain what to do next. But I underestimated her. She suddenly moved. With her leg she kicked out, not too hard, but with enough force to catch the side of Dr Gallows' head and send him off balance. Just in time he grabbed the side of the ladder before he overbalanced, but the force of the blow had made him gasp, and open his mouth. And the package fell. It thunked me on my shoulder as it hurtled past, falling down and down to the bottom of the shaft with a clanking crash. It was lucky that the treasure inside wasn't real.

'Quickly, go, Maisie, go. Get it.' Aunt Hetty called down to me urgently.

I obeyed. I slid, slipped, staggered and fell my way down the ladder. I was excited that I had something else to do. I was quite pleased at how my brain shifted easily back into mission mode now, I thought only about what I'd been told. The muffled curses from Dr Gallows were getting louder, he must have freed his foot and begun to follow. I hit the floor, spotted the package and scooped it up. Backing away from the ladder I shuffled behind the cage into a natural crevice in the wall. It had obviously been hollowed out by years and years of dripping water, eroding the stone and carving out a natural Maisie-sized hiding place. It wouldn't hide me for long, but it didn't need to.

Dr Gallows thumped down, big feet landing heavily on the floor. He stood for a moment, listening, looking all around. But I sat, still as a sloth (I think the saying is as 'still as a mouse' but mice are notoriously scampery so a sloth makes more sense), breathing as shallowly as I could. All I needed was for him to think that I'd scarpered down a tunnel...

'Maisie? Come on Maisie...this isn't doing you any good. Bring me the package and we can get out of here.' Why would he think I'd respond? He must be really desperate, his voice was all whiny. His plans, so carefully laid, were unravelling.

'You've forgotten! You think if you take the treasure then you've somehow won? There is no chance. You have forgotten whose safety hangs in the balance?'

How could I forget that?

'Not your dear Aunt Hetty, but your parents. All I have to do is give word to Luis and Pete, and they can create a tragic boating accident for them. Or a rock fall, or a drowning by freak wave. We can find a way, find a way to end their existence.'

I couldn't let that happen. But I couldn't speak. I waited. Sloths look still but really they're eating or thinking about eating or sleeping or sloooowly moving or thinking about moving. My body was still but my brain was listening and working out what to do next.

'So you have no choice…Maisie? Maisie?' Throughout this rambling ranting, his footsteps had been pacing, pounding the floor, looking this way and that, turning, backtracking, searching for the package, searching for me. He was wrong though. I wasn't stupid. He wasn't about to leave me down here. And if he stayed, there was no way he could get a message to Luis and Pete. No mobile phone would work this far underground. He was stuck. His best chance was to find me and wrestle the package from me in person. I sat in my hollow staring down the dark tunnel facing me, waiting to see if he would come round the cage and spot my hideaway. I was all prepared to fight if I had to. The package was in my right hand, my left was on the ground. I scrabbled, scraped, and then found a perfect-sized stone that fit in the palm of my hand. It was not too heavy to throw, but not so light to be unnoticed. I raised my arm and flung it down the empty tunnel as far and as hard as I could. There was a long long silence, that probably was really a millisecond, and then the pebble struck a wall, rebounding off onto the floor then rattling to a stop. Was it loud enough? Yes! Dr Gallows, hearing the stone spun round and blindly began to hurry down the passageway. He'd fallen, as most people would, for one of the oldest tricks to make someone think you are where you're not, throw something to make a sound somewhere else. It had always been useful if I was hiding up a tree and didn't want to be made to go to bed, I used to throw some of the fruit or a broken branch over to another tree, and my parents would start searching there instead.

As Dr Gallows' back disappeared into the gloom I made my move. I had to choose between moving slow and silent, or fast and loud. I had no time to think either choice through properly, and decided that fast moving was best. Quickly, I darted from the shadows, stuffed the package in the waistband of my trousers, and began to climb. My arms tugged and pulled as my tired legs began to complain, moaning at me for making them climb again. Pushing, hauling myself, I scrambled up as fast as I could. Before I was halfway up, however, I heard Dr Gallows' voice again.

'Just give up. You thought you could fool me, but I can reach you. You would have done better to face me on the ground. Halfway up a ladder, the danger is on your side...' his voice gave up because he could not shout and climb. Even though he wasn't fit his fury was giving him speed he did not have before. And I was so tired. I couldn't look up, couldn't look down, I just moved. Up and up, and all I could hear was my breath, exhausted gasps. Or was that his breath getting closer and louder? I climbed further, harder and felt trapped, as though I was in a perpetual nightmare. Going up the eternal ladder, endless, never reaching the top. On and on and on and I'd be here forever. I felt my determination start to slip away when a hand firmly wrapped itself around mine. And reaching up, looking up, I saw Aunt Hetty reaching down. I pulled myself up to her and out to her, half pulled by her hands, half pushed by my weary legs. Out into the light of the day that blinded me and blocked out any vision of her or the outside world. So much sun in my eyes, it was too much for my head. I shut my eyes as I rolled to the side, out of the way of the opening as she slammed the grille back down.

My eyes were firmly shut and I held my sticky, mucky hands over them. How could something I wanted so much be so horrible to get? When I was in the tunnels, all I wanted was daylight, and now that I had it, all I wanted was to get back in the dark and stop the pain searing through my head. I was lying back on something damp, it was seeping up from beneath, but it was soft, not like the rock I had just spent so long with. Calming down, I took my time trying to get my eyes adjusted, peeking out from one at a time, seeing first blue grey that I thought was sky, then, as I sat up, green and brown and white blurs. I blinked and I could focus. It was hills and grass and sheep. Where was Aunt Hetty?

The voice came from behind. 'No, no, no!' As I turned, eyes wide open at the sound of Dr Gallows' voice, I saw long, filthy fingers sneaking their way through the gaps in the grille from the mine. They were pushing, twisting, trying to get out. But Aunt Hetty's hands were there too, holding it down. And even though Dr Gallows must be stronger than her, he could not force his full weight above his head to lift it off, to move her away. And he was stuck.

Above his yells, Aunt Hetty spoke. 'Listen to me. Listen!' The voice was as commanding as an officer, one she usually reserved for me on my most irritating or mischievous days. One that would reduce me to obedience in seconds. It had the same effect on Dr Gallows, and he was quiet. 'Do you want this package? It's here. Perhaps the contents will still be undamaged, despite their fall. But you will never know unless you listen.'

He was silent. I was silent too.

'I will give you this package, and let you out. But you have to give me the notebook. And you have to let me go.'

'I can just climb back down, go back to the cove. You have nothing on me.' His voice was still breathless from the climb, but menacing all the same.

'You're right.' She was still calm, firm and solid, but calm as the lake near her home. She wasn't scared Aunt Hetty any more, she was as solid as my parents, as brave as anyone else I knew. 'I have little to hold over you, apart from your own greed. You want this package more than anything. And I want my freedom, and I want Gerald to continue his work. I want his notebook, and then I will let you out. You can go. Go far away. I won't go to the police or go to the security services. I don't trust you. If I did that, you'd come and get us, get one of us, get Maisie.'

I didn't want that.

'I cannot and will not risk that. But I'm not letting you go without a trade. The notebook and my freedom for the treasure.'

There was still silence. But not for long. She was so clever, my aunt; she knew that Dr Gallows was all made up of greed and lust. Knew that, ultimately, his desire would prevail over anything else.

'I agree. You will let me out. And then we will exchange…the book for the package. And then you will let me go. The car is there. You will let me go, and not tell anyone.'

He was saying it like it was all his idea. I do that at times. If I get all frustrated and don't know how to do something like mend the strap on my satchel when it snaps, or put a wheel back on a cart if it clatters off down a track, I usually get so mad I can't find any answers. Then someone else comes along (Mum or Dad or Aunt Hetty), talks me into being calm, and then tells me how to sort it. I hate that I didn't know how to do it myself in the first place, so I then repeat what they've told me, but in a way that makes it sound like I came up with the idea. That way I feel more in control of myself.

I wasn't sure that I liked the fact I had something in common with Dr Gallows. Did it make me bad like him? Or did it mean there was a bit of him that was a nice person? It's confusing how there are lots of things that make people so different from each other, but lots of things that make them the same.

Aunt Hetty turned to me. 'Get back, Maisie. You've done your bit. Stay back and keep back. No heroics now. We have to do this.'

She was acting like the treasure was real, like we didn't want to have to give it up. But we knew it was fake, why was she pretending? Then I remembered that Dr Gallows didn't know it was fake, and we couldn't just hand it over without seeming bothered. He needed to believe that it was real. I got excited, because I realised we would end up with more than him, we'd have the notebook and he'd have nothing! My legs jiggled up and down, wanting to skip around, wanting to leap everywhere. We would beat Dr Gallows! But I couldn't, even if I didn't say anything, my leaping across the grass would have seemed a bit odd, and he might have started questioning things. I had to sit tight and pretend like Aunt Hetty. My hands were on the grass. I could feel each tickly prickly leaf poking into my palms. A thought niggled at me, like the blades of grass, prodding at my brain. What would happen when Dr Gallows discovered he didn't have the real treasure? Surely he would then still want to own the real hoard, but also want some sort of revenge, some sort of vengeance. Against us.

Perhaps we should just have given him the real treasure in the first place... I lifted my hands and itched them, scratching away. I wished I could do that in my head. Looking around I could see that we were at the top of a grassy cliff edge, the sea was behind my back and there were lots of sheep (too many for me to quickly count) in the field in front of me. The sheep were munching grass and snoozing like nothing unusual was happening. A rambling footpath cut through the field leading to a dirt track where a black jeep waited, presumably parked there earlier by Dr Gallows or one of his men. This spot was so beautiful if you were a walker, sea bird spotter, a farmer. We were all there though, tired, scared and sore, because of one man's greed. In the adventure books and films, scenes like this always took place in storms with crashing thunder, pouring rain and dark skies. But here the sun shone, the birds shrilled, high-flying above, the sea shook the rocks beneath the cliff. All around us, all the time, good and bad mingle, they mix. Sometimes the edges get blurred, but sometimes we can see good and bad very clearly defined. And we can choose. I knew that we had to take the consequences of what my parents had chosen to do, but that they had chosen to do the thing that was right, the thing that was good.

I watched as Aunt Hetty moved back two steps from the mine shaft. Dr Gallows lifted the grille and up he came. His head, shoulders, chest, legs and feet appeared (one boot unlaced still) and then he was upright, standing, blinking in the sunlight. None of us spoke. He was stooped over, cramped from his climb, but as his eyes adjusted, so did his height, and he straightened up, shoulders back, the confident pose again. He turned to look at Aunt Hetty, ignoring my presence completely. It was as though I wasn't even there, which was good because the less time I had his eyes on me the better. I didn't want Dr Gallows to know anything about me. Reaching under his jumper, he brought forth the red notebook. The cover was scarred, scored, scuffed from its travels and journeys all over the world, the leather worn dark by wear and tear, the sun and the wind. It was my dad's notebook and glorious to see. Dr Gallows handed it over. Aunt Hetty reached out, realised she didn't have anything in exchange and faltered, her hands waving around uselessly in the air. I unfolded my legs, reached for the package at my waist, and went to stand by her. I passed it to her and she passed it across to Dr Gallows. I took the notebook from him, feeling the warmth from the leather on the palm of my hand. It was like holding Dad's hand in mine. I tucked the book into my trouser pocket and zipped it shut, making sure it was safe. Aunt Hetty and I stood side by side as Dr Gallows held the package and looked at us. I braved myself and looked at his face. His eyes were cold dark, like the entrance to the mine that Josie and I uncovered all those hours ago. They were a reminder of what could happen if we went against our agreement.

And then he was gone, striding away towards the jeep, leaving us at the edge of the cliff. And we stayed still as he got in the car, as he drove away, as the dust from the car slowly settled. We stayed still until no trace of his presence on that cliff top remained.

Silently, Aunt Hetty put her arm around my shoulders and squeezed hard. That touch reminded me of what I had found again and I turned and gave her a hug. We stayed there for a moment, but the hug became too tight pushing every bit of me together until I thought I might explode. I stepped back and shook myself off, wiggling space into me again. Together we pushed the grille back onto the shaft, ensuring that any stray sheep wouldn't fall inside or a random rambler slip down and break a leg or two. I felt as though every movement I made was using energy I didn't have, that my arms and legs were crying 'sleep, rest!' to me, just wanting to be still for a bit. I couldn't do that, couldn't shut down. I had to keep going, for a bit longer at least. I looked at Aunt Hetty, she had lots of dust and dirt on her face and clothes and hands. I'd never seen her grubby like that; it was usually me that ended up all messy.

'You look like me!' I laughed.

She looked down at herself and laughed too. 'I suppose I do. Although I'm sure your face is much filthier. We both need a good wash, and you need those scrapes seeing to.'

I'd sort of forgotten my sore bits. I think there were now so many that I just felt an overall ouch and had got used to it.

'Where are we?'

'I think we're on the cliff above the cove where your mum and dad were based. We were trying to work it out when we were down in the shaft. Although the tunnels led this way and that, we've actually ended up pretty much on top of where the entrance is at the sea level.'

'How do we get down to the cove?'

'That I don't know, but if we follow the cliff we should find a path at some point. The question is, left or right?'

We stood facing the sea. There wasn't a wrong choice. It was hard. The word 'right' had more letters in it; 'left' had less. If I chose left, there might be less distance to travel.

'Left.' I made a decision.

'Okay, left it is.'

We walked in silence for a little bit, I wasn't sure what to say. I didn't want to say what I was scared of, in case saying it made it real. But then the words just overflowed out of me without thinking.

'What if…what if the men don't let them go?'

'Luis and Pete? Oh, really, I don't think there's much chance of that. They need to keep your mum and dad alive and exploring. Their aim will be to use your parents again, I'm sure, especially once Dr Gallows realises that the treasure he currently has hold of isn't the real one.'

'But what happens then?'

'Well, with any luck, by that point, your parents will be out of the country and into another one, on another mission, on another trail. And far from the reaches of Dr Gallows.'

'Oh.' Well, that made sense, but the idea of my parents going away again, so soon, and so far, wasn't something I particularly wanted to contemplate. Then a sound caught my ear. The countryside is said to be peaceful but that's not true. I don't think anywhere has no noise, apart from space. I don't like lots of noise but a little bit lets you know that the world around you is still working. In the country there are birds twittering and cawing, the wind whistling, the plaintive baaing or mooing of animals. And here there was also the sea booming and crashing with breaking waves. But the sound I had just heard was different.

'Cooooeeeee.' And then again, 'Cooooeeeee.'

The Australian Aborigines used to use the word 'Cooooeeeee' as a signal to each other when they were out in the bush. I was taught to use it as soon as I could walk given my habit of wandering off and disappearing from my parents' sight. We used it to call to each other wherever we were in the world. In Africa, when I'd gone to watch the warthogs wallowing in mud, a 'Cooooeeeee' would signal to me that it was time for bed. In the Rockies in America when I went to investigate the slice of pizza I had put out as a trap to attract cockroaches to make one into a pet, 'Cooooeeeee' let me know that it was time to go on a bear hunting trip. We used it for everything, anything, to let each other know that we were there. And I heard it now.

'Cooooeeeee,' I yelled back. I called it again, and again. And I heard it again in answer.

'They're down there, they are, I can hear them!' I turned, excitement making me bounce around, leap like a mad thing, like I'd wanted to jump earlier. I'd become a mountain goat, skipping over rocks and tussocks of grass.

'Maisie, calm down – you'll be over the edge of the cliff in a moment. Okay, let's find a path.'

I ran ahead; my tired legs weren't tired any more. They were made strong and alive by the one simple word, that sound that meant so much.

'Here!' I gestured wildly at Aunt Hetty who wasn't moving nearly as fast as me. Adults do seem to be slow sometimes, even when they're excited. I don't want to ever stop being a whirlwind when I'm happy. I'd found an overgrown path that looked like it had once been used by a few very brave sheep, but not for a long time. However, it wasn't impassable. It was not the most sensible route, and it would require concentration and balance, but it was definitely possible.

'Okay. I think we have to try this. But Maisie, take it slowly. The last thing your parents want is bits of you at the bottom rather than a whole person. Remember that. A whole Maisie is better than lots of legs and arms.'

I knew she was talking sense, but it was hard to calm myself down. However, I took three breaths, steadied my hands on my knees which were trembling in excitement, and began to climb down.

Some of it I went frontways, on my bottom, slipping and sliding, using the roots from twisty, prickly gorse to steady my descent, ignoring each prickle into my hands and fingers. Other times, the rockiest bits, I had to do backwards, checking that each foot was steady before I put the next one down. I looked up. Aunt Hetty was following, using my route as guidance. I looked down. I could see the cove. I could see the tent. I could see two people standing at the bottom waiting for me.

I forgot Aunt Hetty's advice. I forgot my own sense. I just forgot everything apart from the fact that my parents were waiting for me. And I let go.

I ricocheted off rocks. Catching my arms, legs, back and head. And then I twisted over, rolling sideways, and thumping off the shale onto the pebbles at the bottom. I lay heaped and stunned. Nothing hurt, but nothing seemed to work. I couldn't think what to say to myself to get myself to move; I'd lost all of my internal instructions. Then someone reached down and picked me up, and I was wrapped tight in four arms, holding me upright.

And I was safe. I had found my home. It wasn't a place, it wasn't a house, it wasn't a room. It was in the arms of people who loved me.

CHAPTER 18

Josie had concussion. I thought concussion was part of an orchestra, but apparently that's percussion and it means drums and cymbals and things. Concussion means your head gets knocked and you go to sleep for a bit, then you wake up and feel ill. But not forever. Josie's okay now. She was in hospital for a while, just to make sure she was going to wake up properly, and now she's staying in Aunt Hetty's house. Not in my room, she's in the one that used to be called the spare room, but now it isn't spare, it's hers. She has to share my bathroom with me and the rubber duck. Like Josie, I had to go to hospital too, but I didn't have concussion, and I didn't have to sleep there. I broke my right and left arms when I did my head-over-heels act at the bottom of the cliff. I feel pretty silly and my arms look massive as they have big casts on them. They're so heavy to lift up but, now that they've stopped hurting, I sort of like the feeling of having my arms tightly squeezed all the time. I'm almost disappointed the casts come off next week, but I can't wait to see just how white and wrinkly my skin is underneath. Josie says they'll look like the arms of a dead thing, and Aunt Hetty just laughs and says that it's a good thing that's the only thing I broke then or I'd really look bad. I got worried until Josie explained my arms wouldn't actually be dead and they'd get back to normal in a few weeks.

Aunt Hetty's looking forward to the fact that I'll be able to do more to help in the house again. I don't think it's been easy for her, having to look after the two of us. I have tried to help, but ever since the disaster when I attempted to do the drying up and she had to buy practically a whole new dinner service, I've been banned from any chores.

That means I've had lots of time to think. I keep asking if Dr Gallows will come back. Everyone says, 'No, we've done what we need to be safe.' Because everyone says it to me, I'm starting to trust them, and starting to believe that it's true. It doesn't stop me worrying, but then I ask again and get the answer and that reassures me for a while. And I've had lots of time to wonder just what is going to happen next. Because Mum and Dad aren't here any more. They've gone again. They had to go. They stayed for a few days, sleeping here in Aunt Hetty's house, spending time with me, going to lots of meetings. I couldn't go too. Even though I'd been in the mines and been part of the adventure, I still wasn't allowed. It didn't seem fair, but they talked to me about what went on, so that I still felt part of things. And then Mum and Dad left.

I know they had to leave. They have to go and follow their next adventure because following adventures is what they do. The night before they left, Dad came to my room and talked to me.

'You see, Maisie, we live here now, today. But people have lived on this earth for so long. And there is so much we don't know, that we need to know, and we need to understand. Not just so that questions from the past are answered, but because if we have some understanding of how we once lived, how we once were, we might be able to make changes that will affect how we are now. Having respect for what was, also gives you respect for what is now. I don't ever want to leave you, but I have to go and continue this work. I can't lie to you, I can't say that there is no danger, but your mum and I need to go.'

I understood. I think. It's like the fact that I'm most comfortable just being me, and just spending time with myself. But I have to spend time with other people, and get to know them, and understand more about them. If I do that then, even though it's hard, I can learn more about myself and actually feel happier. So if Mum and Dad go off exploring, even though it's hard and they might be in danger and they can't always be with me, they can help to find out things that make today's life even better. But I'm still sad that I can't be with them. My arms don't hurt any more – they're nearly mended – but I feel a bit broken inside. Maybe, when these plaster casts come off, and if I really want to, they have said that I can go back to them, go out to wherever they are and join them again.

I'm a Voyager; I want to be part of Voyager adventures. I don't know what I'll decide to do. It will depend on lots of things. But for now, I am still with people who love me, with Aunt Hetty and Josie, and I have another home here. I never thought that a place away from my parents would feel like a place I could truly belong, but I've found that I can belong with other people too. And adventures don't always just happen when you're off investigating other lands. I think I'll see what happens if I stay in this new home of mine for a bit, see what else is here that I can explore.